Shooting from the Heart

MELISSA GABRIEL

authorHOUSE®

AuthorHouse™
1663 Liberty Drive
Bloomington, IN 47403
www.authorhouse.com
Phone: 833-262-8899

Published by AuthorHouse   07/09/2021

ISBN: 978-1-6655-3041-5 (sc)
ISBN: 978-1-6655-3042-2 (e)

Library of Congress Control Number: 2021912943

Print information available on the last page.

This book is printed on acid-free paper.

To Minou Drouet, my first early inspiration,
and others who followed:
F. S. Fitzgerald, E. L. Doctorow, and Anna Quindlen

To my father, Gene Gabriel,
who taught me to love writing

CONTENTS

CHAPTER 1

—₩₩₩～○○₩₩○₩₩○○₩₩—

Sunday-Morning Reminiscence

A shrill whistling invaded Jana's thoughts, jolting her abruptly back to the present. She turned from the window and the glistening snow outside and rushed toward the kitchen to silence the demanding teakettle. The Sunday-morning sun was high in the sky now, streaming across the spacious kitchen. Jana sipped her tea, thinking about how far her life had come from her days in Philadelphia and New York. Gazing at the ocean gave her comfort: it all seemed muted and vague, like something experienced in another lifetime. There was something intangibly serene about living close to the sea. It had taken seemingly eons of time to bring her here at last, and she still could not get enough of it, though she'd been in Newport, Rhode Island, almost a year. The faithful crashing of waves, the screeching of a lone seagull, the far-off foghorns droning intermittently—how she had longed for these sounds and now embraced them fully.

Jana opened the window a crack to breathe in the salty sea air and feel the dampness against her face. Lines she'd once read by an eight-year-old French poet came back to her:

> The sea was there, rubbing against the windows like a huge cat; I opened the window like a chilly kitten; the cat shook her gray tummy, and my face was sprinkled with pleasure, and the hard hand of happiness grasped my heart.

Life was good, so intensely good that at moments like these she feared it might be snatched away. She was still young and beautiful. She couldn't imagine having a more wonderful house. She was self-employed. And she had Michael. Although Michael and Jana had been living together for a little over a year, when she looked into his eyes, Jana still felt that she could not imagine being with a more wonderful man.

———

The elevator opened, and Father Drew quickly emerged and started toward the classroom. Jana stood expectantly as Miranda stopped him. "Father," Miranda said, "this is my friend Jana, who wanted to meet you."

"Well, I hope I'm not too much of a disappointment," Father Drew said with a smile, shaking her hand. He rushed off as Jana stood there unable to respond because of his dazzling looks and charisma. Father Drew was an adjunct professor at St. John's College, and Jana worked there part-time as a secretary. Miranda had been singing his praises for months now, raving about how mesmerizing his sermons were. He was tall with a strong masculine build, wavy black hair, and blue eyes. He worked in Spanish Harlem and had an organization called Full Circle. He was almost always seen with a cigarette and had an intense look of interest on his face when engaged in conversation.

A few weeks later, Jana was at the copier when Father Drew came into the office, leaned over and quickly yet tenderly kissed Sister Paula on the lips. Jana had an orgasm right there at the copier machine.

Father Drew had an office on East Seventy-Second Street in a brownstone in Manhattan. Jana lived in an apartment across the street. It was a time in her life when she was struggling with inner conflicts, and Father Drew slowly became her confidant.

It was the spring of 1969. The Catholic church was emerging from its staid positions, and a new and refreshing breeze was blowing through the portals. Music by the Beatles was played and accompanied by guitar during church services. Flower children flocked to Woodstock, and Peter, Paul and Mary sang "The Times They Are a-Changin'." Protests and marches for freedom abounded. One could feel the energy, and Jana was caught up in the contagion of heady times. Everywhere there was outer and inner turmoil.

Jana's initial visit with Father Drew came about one drizzly spring evening. She called and left a message asking to talk, and they agreed to meet at his office after he returned from a meeting. It grew late, and Jana wondered whether he'd forgotten or just wouldn't show up. But finally a light went on across the street, and her phone rang. She rushed to answer it.

"Hello?" she said tentatively.

"Hello. I'm here. Do you want to come over now?" Father Drew asked.

"OK, if it's not too late."

"No, it's fine."

Jana ran across the street and up the stairs and then rang the bell. They walked into a cozy room with soft lighting, and Jana sat down in a comfortable worn chair, with Father Drew sitting across from her. He lit a cigarette while she began to talk about her troubles with family members. Father Drew meditatively inhaled and exhaled smoke while looking at her and listening carefully. Suddenly he ripped off the white collar and tossed it on the table. Jana was struck by this intimate gesture … of exposure, of vulnerability.

"I think your reaction was completely normal. If you're feeling abused by someone, and it continues, you're going to protest."

Jana had had a huge argument with her mother in which she felt emotionally abused. Yet now she felt guilty about her reaction. They continued to talk, and then Jana thanked Father Drew and left. She felt reassured about her situation and fortunate to have had this time together as she ran across the street back to her place.

"Hey, Jana!" Miranda called as Jana was walking down Seventieth Street toward her.

"Hey what?" Jana said and smiled.

"The Thing in the Spring is coming up soon. Are you going?"

"Yes, I guess. When is it? What is it?"

"It's on Saturday, April twenty-seventh. It's all day, right here on the block—a block party. There are steel bands and kids chalking in the street, food vendors, balloons, and Father Drew gives a talk."

"Do you know what the talk is about?"

"I think it's called 'the good news.'" Miranda stood with a stack of flyers about the Thing in the Spring that she had been distributing around the neighborhood.

The day came, and large pieces of white paper were carefully taped in the street. Chalk was handed out to the children. The steel-band musicians set up their drums. Onlookers began dancing to the music. People dressed up, and balloons were tied to the streetlamps. There was an excitement in the air as Father Drew took the microphone.

"I'd like to start with a poem," he began. "In light, God comes, a gentle beam to pierce imprisoning walls of power and fear. In peace, God comes, a speaker of truth to cleanse subtle makeup that masks us from ourselves. In love, God comes, a contradiction to loosen the bonds we use to hold each other."

And then all eyes were riveted on this man whose charisma appeared to touch many.

CHAPTER 2

New York City in the 1980's

J ana had returned to New York City in the autumn, disillusioned with her career as a social worker and her life in Philadelphia. Through a network of friends, she had been able to land a job as assistant dance instructor at a studio on Fifty-Second and Broadway. The job paid little, but it was still a satisfying beginning. She supplemented her income through solo performances in both ballet and jazz and resumed work as a freelance writer, publishing in mental health journals and as a dance-and-theater critic. The remainder of her income derived from an apartment she sublet for years in Washington Square. Despite a hectic schedule, Jana still struggled financially but was finally doing what she longed to do. She did have other sources of income that alleviated her financial difficulties. Jana's father, Robert Marsh, was a successful novelist and more inclined to lend a hand now that his daughter had left that "tedious profession of social work" and was "pursuing a real career." And there was Jana's circle of friends, several of whom were now successful and happy to take her out for an evening. It had been on just such an evening in late October1983 that Jana met Michael.

Their coming together was in a less-than-romantic fashion. Jana was having dinner with Drew at La Bibliothèque on Forty-Second Street. Michael had been shooting his latest film in the area, and things were going well. He decided to celebrate that night with a close friend, screenwriter David Mitchell. They were seated next to Jana and Drew's table and became jubilantly inebriated after several glasses of champagne. Drew ordered a final manhattan with his usual specifications.

Jana returned from the ladies' room to find Drew engaged in a serious verbal exchange with the waiter. Apparently, there was a bug floating in Drew's manhattan. Michael and David had observed the interaction with the waiter and had begun to commiserate with Drew. Until then, Jana had been unaware of Michael's presence. Her meetings with Drew were always intense because they were so infrequent. Thus, on these occasions, she regarded any intrusion on her time with him with contained hostility. But it was too late—the three men were already immersed in conversation. Drew loved people with a remarkably unconditional regard.

Jana sat working on her composure while becoming increasingly aware of Michael. One could not miss his good looks, but it was his vitality that drew her attention. He had a passion and a confidence that attracted Jana. Alcohol had lowered his customary desire for professional privacy, and he spoke openly and fervently about his latest screen endeavor. Jana felt her attraction mingle with resentment, for she detested the constant flow of filmmakers through the neighborhood, disrupting and rearranging people's lives. She regarded them all as insensitive and inconsiderate, barging their way in with cameras and unmatched arrogance, spending outrageous sums of money to roll the same simple scene a hundred times.

But her thoughts were interrupted as she found all eyes on her and realized Michael was speaking to her.

"Do you live around here, Jana?" Her eyes caught his, and she found herself choosing her words.

"Yes, just next door—in the next building, number forty-five."

She responded to the next customary question: "Well, I—I teach dance, and I'm a freelance writer." She found herself having trouble looking directly at this man; the blood was rushing to her head, her breathing grew harder, and she felt the need to escape. To her relief, Drew stood up then and walked her to her building. The next day, she tried fruitlessly to write and at three in the afternoon went downstairs to collect the mail. There was a card for her at the front desk that read "Michael Wagner, film director, Warner Bros. Productions"—and on the back a note: "Jana, call me at 759-9817 after 9:00 p.m. —Michael."

How flattering! Jana thought. *Should I take him up on his offer and call?* She decided to put the card aside for the moment. A few weeks later, she learned from the Full Circle office that Drew was looking for volunteers to help out in renovating homes in Spanish Harlem. She decided to go up on a Saturday to help out. Drew lived and worked around 110th Street on the east side. Because Drew was loved by so many people, there were many volunteers that Saturday. It was a warm spring day, and Jana, Miranda, and others had discarded their coats while working on sweeping and picking up trash in the abandoned building. After several hours, everyone took a break, and beer and pizza were handed out and gratefully consumed. They worked together for months, almost every Saturday, until there was a break in the work. That last day, in late summer, Jana found Drew standing on the second-floor landing of the semi renovated building. She didn't know when she would see him again. One never knew when he would be available, where he would be traveling, when he would be back. She ached to touch him after all these months. Drew looked at her and then took her in his arms, thanking her for her hard work. *This moment* … Jana thought. This moment she would hold in her memory—the closeness, the touch, the wordless feeling between them—forever, for she did not know when she would see him again.

Back in her apartment in Tudor City, Jana looked for the card from Michael. Finally, she found it and tentatively dialed the number.

"Hello, Michael? This is Jana. We met at La Biblioteque a while ago. You left your card at the front desk of my building."

"Oh, yes! Hi, stranger. How are you?"

"I'm fine. I'm sorry I took so long to call. It's just been a busy time."

"I'm glad you called. I have been thinking about you and wondering if you would like to get together."

"Yes, I'd love to. Are you free tomorrow evening for dinner?"

The two had their first date at Chelsea Place, a restaurant that was a favorite of Michael's. After several dates, Michael invited Jana back to his apartment in Sutton Place. It was a time in her life when her confidence about ever being involved in a healthy and lasting relationship was waning. And then Michael had appeared. Suddenly she felt as though she were a teenager again. Hours of preparation spent in getting ready to see him, endless trips to the bathroom before meeting. There had been something magical between them. The walk up Second Avenue became a ritual. She was unable to concentrate on anything but seeing Michael. A block short of his building, there was an antique shop with a large mirror in the window. There she would pause to glance at her hair and makeup. Upon entering his building, she was greeted by the doorman and then walked the long spacious carpeted hall toward the elevators. Next, a second greeting was exchanged, this time with the elevator man, who took her up to the twelfth floor. Michael would be holding open the apartment door and greet her with a kiss. She knew that part of the mystery of their relationship involved the luxury in which he was surrounded. A luxury she had until then only entered intermittently. Fragmented memories filtered through like clips of film … gray satin sheets, thick piled carpets, the immense tiled bathroom, velvet designer wallpaper, gold-leafed picture frames with individual electric lights, sparkling windows with heavy drapes, and the view—the incredible view of the city. Nighttime was an electrifying spectacle, looking out over the East River at Queens, the horizon twinkling brightly and reflecting its glimmer on the placid water. In those early months, Jana held her breath she and Michael would last. Like other men, he demanded so much. And although she would not admit it, she could not understand what he saw in her. He possessed an incredible degree of energy. Their time together consisted of dining at expensive restaurants, taxiing around to various stores to shop, seeing exhibits, and talking for hours. At his apartment, Michael would sit in his boxer shorts and, for Jana, project on his living room wall reels and reels of film of his favorite and most satisfying achievements. He chain-smoked Marlboro cigarettes and downed endless cups of coffee during those times. Being with Michael was like watching a fascinating and exhausting performance. She wasn't sure whether she would survive to the end. But she had survived; the pace had slackened, and they had grown to know and love each other.

Michael had been thirty-five then and consumed with his work. Success had slowly surrendered itself against his driving persistence. But he found himself alone without anyone to share his good fortune. While his professional security had grown, his prospects for a successful relationship had diminished. His lifestyle was now frantic and pressured with reading scripts, auditioning actors, and arranging sets. Never in one place for very long, he wondered what woman would be willing to accommodate such a life. At moments, he felt an enormous lack of connection. His work demanded so much, gave back so much, yet there seemed to be no time for anything else. He endured the deprivation that success brings, that choice demands. Until Jana, he had to be content with brief interludes of closeness. And even these had been tenuous. Fame had imposed its isolation, and he found himself less carefree and trusting. Walls of precaution had encased him until he began to suffocate.

Initially, Michael looked on Jana as another fleeting anonymous rendezvous. But Jana had been different from other women. She was not the sort one found in Studio 54 or the 21 Club. Most women were impressed by money, power, and good looks, not to mention fame and success. But Jana seemed to look beyond all that. She had a way of persistently chipping away at what one seemed to be, in an intense desire to know what was inside a person. Relentlessly, she peeled away the layers and found inside Michael what was most important to her—the desire and will to give oneself up to life. Both Jana and Michael believed that what was truly significant in life was one's own creativity. Success, money, and power to them were by-products of a far greater achievement, which was the struggle to individually and meaningfully define life. It seemed to them that so many people were engaged in a massive effort to stave off their inevitable deterioration. The 1980s witnessed renewed efforts at reaching optimal health and material success so one could ensure a long and leisurely observation of life. To Jana and Michael, the true enjoyment, the real ecstasy, came in daily exchanging a little chunk of oneself for a turn at life's canvas. It was this essential quality, then, that drew them together. Around it, Jana enjoyed a refreshing independence, and Michael felt free and secure while he was off on location. In this way, they enjoyed time apart to be and grow in their own worlds.

In the time since Jana's return to New York, she worked at an intense pace—writing almost constantly and choreographing and teaching dance. But what the city gave in its unceasing, dazzling excitement it also took with insidious persistence. It was an exhausting courtship that left one ravaged and desolate. Haunted by memories of similar feelings, Jana once again began to feel trapped. Louis Malle in *My Dinner with Andre* had described this feeling of New Yorkers as "guards who had built their own prison and having become both the guards and prisoners they were no longer capable of even making the simple choice to escape." They had all been mesmerized.

When Jana had initially moved into Tudor City in Manhattan, she was in love with New York. The sparkling sidewalks, the side streets of brownstones between Park and Lexington, Second and Third Avenues. She loved the excitement at night, walking home from a friend's at one in the morning and feeling safe. She loved the lit buildings at nighttime, the leisurely days spent in Central Park, the rendezvous with various men in hotels, the nightclub scene, the all-day Sunday mimosa-and-sangria brunches. And, of course, there were the museums and Lincoln Center. But after a while, she began to experience another side of living in the city. Jana reflected on her unhappiness now living in New York City and how she might broach the topic with Michael. Michael had grown up on the West

Coast and always longed to be in New York. He thrived on the city and had lived here for five years.

Jana recalled an evening the week before, when she had been out with Michael.

"Where are we going?" Jana had asked.

"It's a surprise," he'd responded. They arrived at a beautiful romantic restaurant at the Copter Club at the top of the Pan Am Building. Jana was glad she'd dressed accordingly. As the waiter escorted them to a table, Jana noticed the tablecloths were white cotton and candles were lit at each table. Jana had been there a few times with her father.

"It's great, isn't it—the view—don't you think?"

"Yes, Michael, this is fantastic. What's the occasion?"

"There *is* no occasion. I just love the view up here; you can look along Park Avenue and see the glittering lights of the streetlamps for miles. David and I came here a few times when I was on location, and I've always loved it. I wanted to share it with you." Michael flagged the waiter down and ordered a bottle of champagne.

At times, Jana felt Michael excessive but had to admit it was part of the attraction. "Thank you, honey, for bringing me here. It's spectacular."

After the meal, Michael got up and beckoned Jana to the dance floor. Before she knew it, he'd whisked her to the small dancing area, where they were alone, and held her close. They were playing an old song, a favorite back then. "More." Michael swept her around in his arms as people in their seats watched.

"Michael, everyone is watching," Jana said.

"Let them eat their hearts out," he replied.

"Longer than always is a long, long time," the music poured out. In that moment, Jana felt more special than anyone in the room.

After dinner, they returned to Michael's place.

"I have something to show you," he said.

"What is it?"

"You'll see. I hope you like it."

Michael withdrew a shopping bag from the hall closet and told Jana to look inside.

"Michael, this bag is filled with gifts from Tiffany's. Who are they for?"

"For you. Come on—try them on."

They sat on the edge of the bed while she tried on bracelets, necklaces, and earrings.

"Michael, this is too much."

"It's not too much for you, darling. You deserve it, and it makes me happy to do it. You look so beautiful. In fact, I think I must see you naked in your new jewelry to get the full effect."

Michael had pounced on the bed and wrestled with her, laughing, until they had taken each other's clothes off. With their clothes off, Jana initially felt hesitant. It wasn't her first time being intimate with Michael, yet those first few seconds were always uneasy. He moved first, softly kissing her lips and her neck, which always aroused her. They began touching, and Michael slid on top of her, gently entering her. That was the moment of ecstasy for Jana. They'd moved in unison, lost in sensation, peaking almost at the same moment. Michael had rolled over, and they'd both lain quietly, bathed in sweat and sweet satisfaction.

Yes, Jana thought, she would miss the excitement that New York evoked—and particularly evoked in Michael— yet she had made up her mind. How would she tell Michael her feelings? Michael loved New York and thought Jana was having increasing success both as a dance instructor and as a writer. For example, there had been a flattering article in a recent issue of *Dance Magazine*, and she had a regular byline with the *Psychotherapy Networker*. With her success, Michael reasoned that she now had "a foot in the door." But Jana shunned the animalistic competitiveness of New Yorkers. One evening, after an especially hard day at work, Jana came home exhausted and complained to Michael about screeching fire engines, honking car horns, endless lines, and a barbaric city that was sapping her strength. This was not the first time Jana had come home in a tirade of frustration. Michael relented at last, and the following month, they rented a car and drove up to New England to look at houses.

———

The windshield wipers creaked monotonously back and forth as the car crept north along Interstate 95 amid the spring equinox of gusting winds and heavy rain. They rode in silence, the tenor of their feelings as turbulent as the day itself. Jana looked out at the bleak landscape and wondered whether people were more vulnerable out in the elements or during those moments when they felt utterly estranged from those closest to them. Michael had been in a foul mood from the start. He now had to postpone shooting for at least a week.

Michael could neither understand nor fully accept

17

Jana's urgency to leave New York. He resented her for creating an unnecessary upheaval in their lives and expressed his annoyance in his customary manner by withdrawing. This took the form of meditatively inhaling and exhaling cigarette after cigarette with a fixated stare on the road ahead. Jana hated these times when Michael was angry. She felt guilty and vulnerable to his moods and in desperation tried to focus her thoughts on something comforting. She soon fell asleep to the sound of Vivaldi's *Four Seasons* lulling because it had become as familiar to her as Tchaikovsky's ballets and no longer held her attention. But it was one of Michael's favorites. He carried an assortment of classical music on a single CD with him everywhere: "In a Persian Market," "Meditations from Thais," and *The Four Seasons*. Each held a special significance. Michael's first girlfriend had loved "Persian Market." He had heard "Meditations" through headphones on a red-eye flight from California and instantly fallen in love with the piece. And Vivaldi's *Four Seasons*—Michael's mother loved Vivaldi.

He felt the urge to lean over and close his hand over hers but instead lit another cigarette and asked himself how it was that women developed such a talent for being so wearing at times. Why did they always persist in fighting against the flow of life? No situation ever seemed to be quite right for them. He had enough on his mind now without the added pressure of looking for a house, a new town in which to live. How simple and convenient it seemed to fly into New York, a major airport, catch a taxi, and be at the apartment in less than an hour. Living in New England would mean flying into Boston or Providence and driving to whatever town in which they settled. Michael exhaled a long stream of smoke. On the other hand, he could not stand to see Jana suffer and knew she could no longer bear to remain in the city.

They had been given a few recommendations from friends about various towns, especially artsy ones and those close to the ocean. They stayed in hotels in a few towns and visited some scenic places. But finally, although more of a distance from New York than Michael wanted, they decided on a house along Ocean Drive in Newport, Rhode Island. In late May, Michael sold his apartment, Jana gave up hers, and they settled into their new home. While each preferred the more charming older homes, they selected a newer modern house primarily because Michael was often away and neither wanted to deal with repairs. The house looked east facing the ocean, set back about five hundred yards from the road. Rambling green lawns surrounded the houses, and by comparison, theirs was modest in size.

CHAPTER 3

Life in Newport

J ana leaned over and allowed the hot spray of the shower to pound against her neck and shoulders. She had found a wonderful dancing school in town and ached from a difficult ballet class taken the day before. She decided to take the intermediate class for instructors, which worked every muscle in her body. Now, as steam filled the room, her mind went over the week's schedule. There was the audition for the Charleston clip of the *Great Gatsby* movie being filmed at Rosecliff, a deadline for an article she was writing on movement therapy for children with disabilities, the carpet shampooers on Tuesday, the housekeeper on Wednesday, and Michael's return from filming in New Mexico on Thursday. Saturday evening, they would be entertaining local friends. As she dressed in the bedroom, Prokofiev's Classical Symphony no. 1 in D played on the radio. Jana smiled, recalling this as the first music she'd choreographed in college. She slapped lotion over her legs and barely waited for it to dry before hurriedly pulling on pantyhose and shorts. The dress requirement for the Charleston audition was shorts, clear stockings, shoes with medium heels, and a T-shirt. Chilly, Jana tugged at her black leg warmers, pulling them over her thighs.

At the Rosecliff Mansion on Bellevue Avenue, there was an abundance of cars, trailers, and people associated either directly or marginally with the *Gatsby* shooting. Fortunately, professional dancers were auditioned prior to the general crowd, so Jana did not have a long wait. The casting director was short, in his fifties, with curly black hair, and wore a lavender leotard with gray sweatpants. Mr. Martins reminded Jana of one of her dance instructors in NYC with whom she had studied jazz, and this likeness relaxed her when her turn came.

"Next!" barked Mr. Martins. "Up here. Line up in fours—five rows, please!"

Despite Jana's experience, she felt a bit of nerves. The women ran through the routine. After only a minute or two, Martins pointed to individuals and barked, "You, you in the last row, you in the middle front row. The rest, thank you."

After a short wait, Jana was told she'd made the cut and left in good spirits.

It was shortly after ten o'clock when Michael turned the car onto Ocean Drive and made his way through the misty, windy night along the winding road that led home. To his right, the ocean surged up over the rocks in a mighty spray, meeting the damp drizzle. Although tired from the flight and chilled by the sudden temperature change, he felt that contented satisfaction one experiences in completing a task that measures up to one's expectations. Only a nagging ache in the middle of his back reminded him of the strain of the last few weeks. Despite the fact that he would have to resume shooting in a week, Michael savored the respite from work. His thoughts turned to Jana, and a flood of warmth filled his veins. God, she was beautiful; he could see her thick brown hair and firmly curved dancer's body, her brown eyes that shined back at him and that throaty laugh. He also recalled the qualities that had initially attracted him: her wit and sense of humor, intelligence, playfulness, sensitivity, but perhaps most how completely and fathomlessly she seemed to love him.

Before Michael set his luggage in the front hallway, Jana raced toward him, circled her arms around his neck, and hugged him tightly. She looked like a teenager in her white T-shirt and red bikini underwear.

In her customary rush, she began, "How was New Mexico and the flight home? God, you've got a great tan. I made the Charleston clip! Don't forget we're having company this weekend."

This flood of words was accompanied by another customary habit she had on his returns, of dancing about him as he made his way through the house to the bedroom. Michael ended this exuberant monologue by taking her in his arms and kissing her.

"Hi, honey," he finally said. "Is there any coffee? It's freezing in here."

Next to the warmth of the fireplace, Jana lay with her

head in Michael's lap as he recounted the progress of the past three weeks.

"Jana, the sunsets of New Mexico are simply spectacular. The cinematography is going to be outstanding. Pamela Curry was definitely a wise choice for the lead. She is amazing, and Daniel is great with her. In fact, everyone is working well together. But the heat was unbearable some days, and everyone was complaining. The makeup people were getting frustrated with retouching, so I decided we could all use a break.

"I missed you. I brought you something."

"What did you bring me?" Jana asked and smiled, looking up into his face.

Michael reached into his pocket and withdrew a small box inside of which lay a Mexican turquoise stone ring, which he held out to her.

"Oh, Michael," Jana exclaimed. "It's beautiful. Thank you."

That night, Jana massaged Michael's back, and with the window slightly ajar, they made love to the sound of the waves crashing against the wet sand. The next morning, Michael slept while Jana puttered around the house and prepared breakfast. Rosa, the housekeeper, had already done all the heavy cleaning. Things were reasonably organized since their move, though much remained to be done. Michael emerged from the bedroom, his dark brown hair tousled, a comforter wrapped around his shoulders, and he made his way to the kitchen, where the smell of fresh coffee drew him.

"Jana, honey, we have to talk," Michael began.

"Good morning," Jana replied.

"Good morning," Michael repeated as an afterthought. "I don't mind having our friends to visit. I just don't understand why they have to visit after I've just gotten home and there's so much we still have to do around here."

They discussed the issue of Michael's discomfort with having visitors so soon, and ultimately Michael resigned himself to Jana's plans. After breakfast, Jana stole a few hours away and drove to Fort Adams State Park to walk along the grounds and be with her thoughts. When she returned, there was a phone message from Drew asking whether she had settled in all right, an unexpected delight.

CHAPTER 4

~~~ɯvɔɢɘɤɔɢɤɔɔɔvɯ~~~

On Location

A month had passed, with Michael returning to Santa Fe to continue directing his film. Jana's closest friend, Camille, had telephoned to say she would need to reschedule her visit to Newport. At loose ends, Jana decided to fly to New Mexico to visit Michael and see the set of his film. As the plane made its ascent, Jana leaned back in the seat and opened a chocolate-covered wafer candy bar made by De Beukelaer, which was her favorite. She always got them at a newspaper stand on Sixty-Eighth Street and Lexington Avenue when living in the city. She savored the recollection. In a few hours, she would be in New Mexico. She closed her eyes and relished the relief of no responsibilities for a while, of the chance to do some sightseeing and enjoy visiting Michael. For a time, Jana read and allowed her thoughts to drift. She soon fell asleep but was awakened after a short nap to the sight and smell of a hot meal. Glancing around, she noticed an attractive woman seated across the aisle. She couldn't help noticing what beautiful skin she had, a golden brown—and long black hair. She was wearing an emerald-green suit with white trim and white heels. A white straw hat rested on the seat beside her. She returned Jana's glance, and Jana saw that she had bright emerald-green eyes.

"This is my favorite part of the flight—mealtime," laughed the lady in green, revealing even white teeth.

"Yes, I know what you mean," Jana replied. *She must be a model*, thought Jana.

"Where are you headed?" the woman asked.

"I'm landing in Albuquerque and then heading to Santa Fe."

"Oh, so am I! My brother lives there and we try to visit each other at least once a year. I do have an ulterior motive, though. I adore coming out and experiencing this city. By the way, I'm Leah."

"I'm Jana. My boyfriend is a film director on location, so I've come to spend some time with him. He raves about how beautiful it is, and now I'll have a chance to see if he's exaggerating," Jana laughed.

The women chatted for a while. Leah recommended places to visit, sights to see. She told Jana about the Southwest Indian art and the museums and restaurants she and her brother enjoyed. As the plane descended, Leah and Jana exchanged numbers, with plans to meet during Jana's stay. Driving from the airport, Jana could see the high range of mountains in the background and a wide expanse of blue sky. As they passed, she noticed the Pueblo-style architecture and adobe homes. During the drive, the taxi driver told Jana that if she enjoyed museums, an interesting one to check out would be Georgia O'Keeffe's.

The Hotel Santa Fe was in the heart of town. Once inside, Jana looked with pleasure around the room. It was arranged in pink and beige, with thick piled carpet that her toes sunk into. The bedspread was of small pink flowers against a cream background and was thick and puffy, with a lace bed skirt and several throw pillows. The curtains were sheer beige and shimmered in the sunlight. Oak furniture with American Indian pottery in turquoise and cream adorned the tables. The hum of the air conditioner gave a peacefulness to the room. Jana puttered around unpacking while wearing an oversized white terry cloth robe. Despite the warm weather, she drew herself a hot bath and added some scented oils. She could use a relaxing bath.

There was a message from Michael to call when she arrived. Her heart raced a bit; after all this time, she still became excited at the prospect of seeing this man. She picked up the phone and dialed. Doing so, she thought of all the men she had made love to in hotel beds—the various places, various circumstances. It was good to be with one person.

"Jana? Hi, hon. How was your trip?"

"It was wonderful! The mountains from the plane were spectacular! I made a friend and may get together with her for lunch. She is also a dancer like me so we have something in common."

"That's great! Do you want to come out to the set for a tour?"

Michael sent a car for her. The location was just north,

29

on the way to Nambe and Chimayo. Jana really didn't know much about Michael's current movie. She knew only that it was a project he wanted to work on for a long time. The story line centered on a married law professor who falls in love with a Native American girl at his law firm.

As the car turned into the parking lot, Jana's anticipation grew. There was a group of trailers in a big circle, which reminded her of a wagon train. Equipment was everywhere. People were everywhere, running hurriedly around making adjustments on the set.

"Well, this is our home away from home, Ms. Marsh," announced the driver with a smile. "I'll take you over to Mr. Wagner."

Michael held out his arms to embrace Jana and hold her for a moment. She could smell his familiar scent, Paco Rabanne, which she breathed in deeply. She took a long look at him, dressed in khaki pants and a light blue shirt and wearing dark glasses. *How handsome he is!* she thought.

"Hi, darling. It's wonderful to see you. I've missed you." He leaned over and gave her a kiss on the cheek. "Are you thirsty? Would you like something to drink?"

"Yes, that would be great. It's really hot here!"

As there was a break in the schedule, Michael took this opportunity to show her around. They were filming on an open arid area of land about fifteen minutes from the city. They walked over to Michael's trailer. Jana carefully surveyed his home away from home. It wasn't the most organized place, but it had all the amenities one could ask for. There was a bedroom / living room area, a small kitchenette, a bathroom, and an area where Michael went over his work at the end of the day. The refrigerator was stocked with lots of drinks, fruits, and snacks.

Michael came up behind Jana as she was examining the trailer and put his arms around her waist. She could feel him getting hard as he began to kiss her neck. Her head went back, and she moaned with pleasure. She turned and put her arms around him. They held each other for a minute and savored this closeness in the way that one savors extra minutes in bed in the morning, holding on to each second, lengthening the seconds into minutes, until Jana gently moved away and urged Michael to show her the rest of the set before he had to go back to work.

She marveled at how everyone worked so hard in the extreme heat. There were sun umbrellas over the actors' and director's chairs and coolers perched near them. The scene they were about to shoot took place outside the "law office" with the law professor about to ask his paralegal out for a drink. Jana watched as Michael set the scene. She could see why he loved his work. There was an electricity and energy that the cast and crew generated as they prepared for action. After meeting the cast and watching for a while, Jana decided to take the car back to the hotel. Before she left, Michael explained that he did not expect to get much time off from working and hoped perhaps she could connect with some guided tours. He motioned to one of the staff nearby.

"Hey, Jeff," he called out. "You're familiar with the tours in town. Do you know of a company Jana could call to arrange a guided tour?"

Jeff took off his cap and wiped the sweat from his brow

as he considered the question. "Sure, I know a few I can write down for you," he answered amiably.

Jana thanked him and put the list in her bag and then returned to the hotel.

Toward the end of the afternoon, the wind blew up fiercely, making work impossible. Michael wiped the dust and soot from his forehead, neck, and throat. The cameraman, Stu, complained to Michael that the lens kept clouding up. So they called it quits. Michael did not bother to shower. All he could think of was getting back to the hotel as soon as possible and being with Jana. For weeks, he had lain in bed at night and thought about holding her in his arms. He suddenly had the feeling one has when very close to experiencing something wonderful—that somehow obstacles would appear to thwart his goal of getting to Jana. He laughed then and thought of what an incurable romantic he was. She had no idea how lonely he grew at times without her. It wasn't just the lack of physical comfort he missed but the support of a listening ear and someone with whom to share his days. He realized now that to have Jana with him, alongside him in something he felt so passionate about, was the ultimate joy.

When Michael opened the hotel-room door, Jana was putting the finishing touches on her makeup. Her heart skipped a beat. Michael came to the bathroom door and looked at her reflection in her mirror. She was breathtaking. With his eyes, he traced the ends of her shoulder-length hair, then the length of her slender arms, all the way down to her beautiful long fingers and the diamond ring on her left hand. She wore a black dress with thin shoulder straps and an emerald heart necklace, a gift for their first anniversary. He leaned over and kissed her, sneaking a glance in the mirror at her face.

"Honey, I am so hungry. I hope you know where we're going to eat." She smiled at him wryly.

"OK, I get the message. You want to eat first. I wouldn't want you to go for more than a few hours without food. I know how grouchy you get," he said and grinned.

"Not to mention the fact that you desperately need a shower," Jana added.

Michael took a long hot shower and got ready to go out. They went to a small Italian restaurant that Michael had selected. Not particularly glamorous, but it afforded a good deal of privacy—and their table was in an alcove. They held hands, kissed, and talked quietly, catching up on each other's news. Michael confided to Jana how much he had missed her. On the way home, Jana talked about meeting Leah on the plane. Michael suggested she take Leah up on her invitation and call her so she would have company while he was working. They went to bed early, wanting time to rediscover each other.

Over the next few days, Michael left for location early while Jana toured the area. She visited the national forest on a guided tour. She went to a few museums and sampled the food at cafés and stands. Occasionally her thoughts wandered to Drew; she wondered what he was up to and cherished past memories. After one of her excursions, Jana returned in the late afternoon for a short nap. She'd bought Michael a beautiful shirt handwoven by the Hopi tribe and smiled at the thought of pleasing him with this gift. Just then, the phone rang.

"Jana? This is Leah. Is this a bad time?"

"Oh, no. I'm so glad you called. How are you?"

"Great. How is Santa Fe treating you?"

"Well, it's exciting, different, fun. And of course seeing Michael every day is great! It's a bit lonely sometimes during the day, though. Why don't you join me for lunch one day?"

"I'd love to. In fact, the reason I'm calling is to ask if you'd be interested in going to the ballet. There's an excellent local ballet company that has matinee performances I think you would enjoy. My brother has no interest in ballet, so I usually wind up going alone."

"That sounds wonderful! When are they performing?"

"There's a matinee performance this Wednesday. I know a wonderful spot to have lunch if you like Mexican food, and then we could see the performance."

"Perfect. How far away are you from the Hotel Santa Fe?"

"Just a few minutes. I'll come by and pick you up around eleven thirty. How's that?"

"OK, good. I'll look forward to seeing you—and by the way, I love Mexican food!"

Jana smiled at the thought of spending the day with Leah. It would be nice to have someone to chat with who knew her way around. When Michael returned that evening, his spirits were sagging. Not even the surprise of Jana's gift made him perk up. Shooting had been painfully slow. He was falling behind schedule and afraid of running over budget. He would probably wind up having to stay in

New Mexico another month or so, and everyone on the set was complaining. Jeff, the makeup artist, became annoyed when the wind caked the made-up faces with sand. Jana tried to distract Michael by recounting some humorous events from her day. She imitated two elderly southern ladies bargaining with a salesman at an outdoor craft fair. They wore great broad straw hats of pastel colors to protect themselves from the sun.

"What y'all want for that necklace?" the one in the pink hat had asked. When the merchant told her, she turned to her friend.

"Vera, did you hear that? My heavens! What is the world coming to when people want more for a necklace that you'd pay for a month's groceries?"

The lady in blue clicked her tongue in agreement. They shook their heads and gave the salesman admonitory looks. Then they'd stood there as if waiting for him to apologize.

Michael smiled weakly. "I'm going to take a quick shower, hon." He let the hot spray beat against his back. Michael had a secret he needed to share with Jana. He thought now might be an ideal time but realized there was never a good time. He dreaded the idea of even broaching the topic and lapsed into more pleasant thoughts of the comfort of her presence and companionship.

"Let's order in tonight, Jana. Do you mind?"

"Not at all. I've been walking around all day. Dinner here sounds wonderful."

"They don't have a terrific selection, but we can get some burgers or salads. Their desserts are pretty good."

They had a quiet dinner and settled into bed early,

watching a movie. There was only so long Michael could put off telling Jana what he must, but right now, lying with his arms around her, it was easy to forget and bask in the blissful security of her love and affection.

On Wednesday, Jana waited outside the main hotel entrance under the canopy as it poured outside. She tied the belt of her raincoat tighter. Thought it was warm, the dampness seeped through her. A black Saab zipped up to the curb, and Leah rolled the window down.

"Hi!" Leah called out.

Jana jumped in the front seat. "I'm so glad you called me. It was a perfect idea to see a local ballet."

Jana and Leah had discovered on the plane that both were dance instructors. Although Jana taught only part-time, Leah was a full-time instructor at two schools in Massachusetts. She told Jana that her late parents were from the Cape Verde islands and had settled in southern Massachusetts. They lived in a sort of enclave with other Cape Verdeans, and she and her brother, Marcus, were from a close-knit family.

"When I was a little girl," Leah told her, "there was a ballet-dancing studio on the same street as my house, and I began taking classes when I was four. My cousins joined for ballet, tap, and acrobatics, but I was the only one to keep up with it."

They turned into the parking lot of Los Amigos and found an empty space. It was crowded, but fortunately Leah had reservations. As they walked, Jana noticed Leah had typical dancer's legs: long with narrow ankles, set off beautifully by her black-and-white heels. Dancers noticed these things about one another; it came from spending years in dressing rooms comparing notes from the time they were children. Leah wore a smart-looking black-and-white suit, and Jana was a little jealous of her tall slender figure. The feeling evaporated quickly as Leah smiled warmly across the table.

"What do you think? I always make a point of coming here at least once when visiting Marcus. If you like Mexican food, it's one of the best. I recommend the chicken enchiladas."

"It smells delicious," Jana replied. "We don't have many Mexican restaurants in Newport."

"By the way, the ballet is a combination of some popular pieces: Tchaikovsky's waltz from *Swan Lake*, the 'Love Theme from *Romeo and Juliet*,' and 'Morning' from Peer Gynt Suite."

"What a great combination! I love those pieces. I did some choreography using some of those once."

The two women chatted about their experiences as instructors and the teachers they both knew from the New England area, and gradually the conversation turned to places Jana had visited in Santa Fe.

"It sounds like you've hit the major attractions already," Leah laughed. "You're more ambitious than I am! If you get a chance to go back to the Southwest Craft Market, there's a wonderful display on an artist who paints dancers in various mediums."

"Oh, I would love to see that!" Jana exclaimed.

They finished their meal and left for the concert. Jana thought how vibrant and upbeat a person Leah seemed to be and was grateful for the company. She hoped they might become friends. They settled into their seats, and

Jana waited with anticipation for the ballet to begin. As she listened to the familiar music and watched the young dancers, something stirred deep inside her. A remembrance, perhaps, of years earlier, when she, too, could create magic on the stage. The performance was better than Jana had expected, and the dancers received a rousing applause.

Afterward, the women decided spontaneously to go out for a drink. Jana shared with Leah that years before, when she lived in New York City, she had subscriptions to the American Ballet Theater and to the New York City Ballet. She and friends would go for drinks on Saturday afternoons after the performance, and she missed those days. Dodging raindrops, Jana and Leah made their way into a small café near the theater. Over amaretto on the rocks, they shared their reactions to the performances.

"When are you going back east?" Leah asked.

"I guess in a week or so. I have classes that someone is covering and some articles to get out within deadline. Michael thinks he will be delayed for another month, which will be hard on us," Jana sighed, "but I do miss being home. What about you? How long will you be here?"

"Probably not long. I get bored easily. I need adventure!" Leah replied with a warm, easy laugh. I'm on a break anyway. Classes don't begin for another month, so there's no rush."

They talked about how fortunate they'd been to meet on the plane. Jana thanked Leah again for inviting her to the ballet and suggested they try to do something again before she left. They decided on a museum later in the week, and Leah dropped Jana at the hotel.

Back in her room, Jana put the television on for company. Michael was usually back by now, and Jana did not know if his delay was a good or bad sign. She called her friend back east to catch up on the news. No one made Jana laugh like Camille. She felt they were like sisters—or the closest she would get, not having any herself. By the time they'd exhausted their stories, Michael came in, and Jana noticed a strange look on his face, like that of someone who knows a wonderful secret and is not about to part with it. In the next second, he slid his hand under her and lifted her in his arms, twirling her around the room loudly singing opera. Jana remembered then why she was with him. It was because of unpredictable moments like these. He covered every inch of her neck with kisses before putting her down.

"What's all this about?" Jana asked.

"I had the most wonderful day of shooting. The actors were brilliant, the crew worked hard, and it was productive and satisfying, and—and because I love you. Do you know how beautiful you are, my love?"

"Wow," Jana replied. "I wish all your days would be like this one."

"Yeah, me too. We may even have cut some time off the schedule. So where do you want to go tonight? Your choice."

"Actually, I'd love a good steak," Jana replied.

"Oh, that's easy!"

They drove to a place not far from the hotel. At the restaurant, Michael reached across the table and held Jana's hand. He lit a cigarette and exhaled slowly and then ordered a bottle of expensive red wine. Suddenly, Michael felt so lucky—about having Jana, a wonderful career, enough money. He cherished her. He didn't know why he'd ever thought about telling her something from the past, something that could disrupt, maybe even damage, what they had together.

He was content to just sit and stare into her eyes, like teenagers do. And he knew she adored him. He talked animatedly about the film and what he had learned as a director from this movie. Michael sensed that Jana was proud of him, and a surge of well-being flooded his body.

"Darling," he said, "I'm so glad you came out to see me. It's been wonderful. I'm going to miss you when you go. I'm spoiled now."

The next day, they decided to spend the day sightseeing together. Michael called the set and conferred with Jeff and the rest of the team about what needed to get done that day. Jana took Michael back to the craft festival so she could see the paintings of the ballet dancers Leah had mentioned. The two went from one art exhibit and craft tent to another, walking everywhere. It was a sunny day with a slight breeze, and they spent as much time outdoors as possible. By evening, they were exhausted.

The remainder of Jana's vacation went by like a whirlwind. Michael surprised her with little gifts that she had admired when they were out. They visited with a few of Michael's coworkers for dinner. She saw Leah one afternoon, and before she knew it, was on the plane headed east.

CHAPTER 5

Camille

J ana arrived home to find that the deadline for a dance critique article was almost upon her. She decided to go to the library to write, as she found she was able to concentrate better in a more confined setting. After she had written for about an hour, her mind began to drift to thoughts of time spent in libraries past. Hours of time she'd clocked studying in college and in graduate school. But there had been time for romances, too, she recalled with a smile. Times when she sat behind someone in the stacks or across from someone at the table and found it hard to concentrate. She thought fondly of those days and those loves, of running to get sandwiches for a college sweetheart who was "imprisoned" in the library for a week one summer. Or just the satisfaction she derived from being near someone with whom she was in love.

Drew had been the first person with whom she'd actually fallen in love. She thought back nostalgically to the last time she'd seen him and felt some sadness. She thought of having loved many men whose images paraded before her—celebrations of love that were like giant fireworks in her life and some, perhaps, that could have been saved, but she had been too careless. Some nothing could have saved. She was more careful now.

Jana awoke from her reverie to see that it was already dark. She hurried home to make dinner and type up the article to get it out in the morning mail. The next day, she left for rehearsal at Rosecliff for the first day of shooting for the Charleston clip. She drove along Bellevue Avenue past the spectacular mansions, called "summer cottages" back in the day. She pulled into the enormous driveway at Rosecliff still finding it hard to believe that she actually had a small part in a major motion picture. In the dressing room, she saw Julie, a dancer acquaintance who had also made the clip.

"Hi, Julie! How are you? Have you been holding down the fort?"

"Hey, girl, where have you been? Martins is totally nuts. I mean, he is working us to death. He thinks the intermediate class is the advanced. Last night, I had to soak in the tub for an hour!"

"Ugh! I'm glad I missed that. Well, hopefully today should be fun."

"I heard that Martins is a perfectionist and that he can sometimes keep you twice as long as a shoot needs to take. I'm not up for being here every day for months. I mean, get a grip."

Jana laughed. Julie had a very colorful way of speaking that amused her.

"I was in New Mexico visiting Michael. This was my first time out west, and it was amazing seeing the sights, especially the majestic beauty of the mountains. Of course, it was great to see Michael as well. I'm kind of glad, to tell you the truth, for the rehearsal time coming now. It gets lonely sometimes without him."

"Well, come on, girlfriend. I'll keep you company."

The choreographer blocked out the routine with the dancers, and they ran through it a few times. Julie entertained everyone by improvising the parts she didn't know yet. They rehearsed on the huge back patio of the mansion, with its view of the ocean in the distance. When they finally quit for the day, the group decided to go and get something to eat. They chose Yesterdays, which had been in Newport for seeming eons, outliving other restaurants that came and went. It was known for catering to the artsy crowd, dancers, writers, and painters. The women found a corner booth and crowded in together. They studied the menus, and Jana selected a grilled-chicken salad and an iced tea. Everyone had built up an appetite from the vigorous workout. After they ordered, the conversation turned to talk of rehearsal.

"How long do you think the whole clip will take?" Wendy asked.

"Who knows? At least he wasn't as bad as I expected him to be today," Gwen added.

"The costumes are pretty cool."

"I know. And we look awesome in them!" Julie remarked.

"This is such an opportunity for us. Just think—we are now stars of the Charleston scene in the *Great Gatsby* filmed in Newport, Rhode Island, and everyone will read our names in the credits of the movie!" Jana exclaimed.

"You are so out of touch with reality," Julie said. "As if people really bother to read all the credits."

"Well, this won't look too shabby on our résumés," Jana replied.

The food arrived, and the group fell silent, satisfying their hunger. Afterward, they ordered coffee and tea and chatted about the stars, the director, working conditions, and the musicians. When Jana looked at her watch, it was almost eight o'clock. She dashed home to find three messages on her home phone. One was from Michael; one from her cousin Adrienne; and one from her best friend, Camille. She decided to call Camille first. As it turned out, Camille was available to travel to Newport the coming weekend. Camille had a co-op apartment in one of the best areas of Brooklyn and was divorced and about Jana's age. They'd met many years before, when Jana was still a social worker, and had been friends ever since. Camille called to say that her relationship with Frank was running into problems and she wanted to talk to Jana. She also was eager to see Jana's new digs. Despite Camille's problems, she was always able to laugh at herself and life. She and Jana enjoyed each other's company. It was the kind of relationship where they could tell each other everything and be themselves. With the plans set, Jana called Michael, who reported that they were pressing on with the film, slowly but surely getting through. Finally, she left a message on Adrienne's voice mail that she was hoping to make a trip to New York City very soon.

The remainder of the week progressed peacefully. Jana

went to rehearsal, and the group went out to eat afterward. She worked on a few articles and looked forward to Camille's arrival. She went grocery shopping to get some of Camille's favorite things. Rosa, the housekeeper, came one day and cleaned. Rosa was a hard worker and good natured. She was from Portugal originally and had come highly recommended.

On Friday, Jana picked Camille up from the train station in Kingston. The ride was about four hours from New York City, and the train had been crowded. Nevertheless, Camille was in good spirits.

"So I was checking out some of the cute guys, businessmen types," Camille began. "Before you know it—never fails—I'm sitting surrounded by about three or four men hanging on my every word! I was the life of the party. One guy said that the trip never went so quickly! I had everyone laughing, as usual."

"I always say that you missed your calling in life as an entertainer. Now give me a hug! I thought we could get some take-out food on the way home and eat in if that's okay. What do you think?"

"Perfect! Do they have any ethnic restaurants, like Mexican or Indian?"

"Yes, we are not exactly in the boondocks. Newport is quite a cosmopolitan town!"

"Good, then let's get Mexican!"

Jana still could not believe that Camille was really here. She gave her a brief tour of the town, around Ocean Drive, along Thames Street, and then up to Memorial Boulevard to a local Mexican place that was a favorite of hers. Although it was early May, the weather was cold and damp by the time they arrived home, so Jana lit a fire, and they sat around the coffee table eating their takeout.

"Wow, this is pretty cool, looking right out at the ocean. Maybe I'll come up more often."

"Wait until you see it by daylight. It's still breathtaking to me even though I've been here for a while now."

They devoured their food while catching up on each other's news. Jana brought out homemade margaritas with lots of salt, Camille's favorite. After a few drinks, they broke down and had a couple of cigarettes, an old vice and semi ritual.

"So when is Michael coming home?"

"I'm hoping it won't be too much longer. I can't sleep well when he's not here. I think every little sound, which is mostly the wind, is someone breaking in. If it weren't for rehearsal, it would be really lonely."

"You love it when he's not here! You like to do your own thing anyway. You always say you need a lot of space."

"Yeah, but I'm used to living with Michael now."

They stayed up until around one in the morning, smoking, drinking, and sharing confidences. Jana even confided in Camille that she was attracted to Drew and missed the days when she had worked with him. Finally, they decided to call it a night and Jana showed Camille to the guest room. Then she staggered into bed herself. In the morning, Jana found Camille already up and fixing coffee.

"You're right—this is some view. Jana, this is so fabulous. How did you find this place? Not that I would ever consider leaving New York, but it *is* beautiful."

"I knew that if we could afford it, I wanted to live on Ocean Drive. I just never thought we would be able to, and then we found this house on the market. It had been vacant a while. I guess it was just timing. Every day, I sit here in the kitchen drinking my morning coffee, Cam, and look out at that sea. I never get tired of it. It has so many different faces and is so restorative."

"Well, I think I would get bored, personally, living up here. Don't you miss the city?"

"Sure, at times. But I can always go down when I want. I can enjoy the fun of New York without putting up with the unpleasant aspects. Anyway, I'll never regret leaving. It was the best decision I ever made."

Camille and Jana spent the afternoon shopping along Brick Market Place and Thames Street. It was mild out, and they walked down by the harbor to sit for a bit and watch the activity.

"You're so lucky you have done something with your life," Camille began. "You have a couple of careers, and you're successful at them, and you have a great guy. Sometimes I feel like I haven't done anything with my life."

"But how can you say that? You have a son who goes to the smartest school in New York City and is in the top of his class. Raising a child to be successful in this world is a huge accomplishment. Look at what Gary has achieved!"

"You really think so? I guess, and I am really proud of him, but I still feel unfulfilled at times. Everyone tells me I should have been a comedian, an entertainer ... well, maybe in my next life!"

"Despite having Michael and knowing Drew, my career, all of it ... I still feel, Camille, at times, that there is something missing from my life, a longing for something I can't quite explain. It's just there in the distance, haunting me—stalking me, almost."

"Really? You never told me that. I would never have guessed that about you."

In the evening, they went to dinner at Christie's and then for a drink at the Red Parrot, where every decadent dessert imaginable was on the menu. When they arrived home, they changed into pajamas, getting comfortable for another long chat into the night.

"So tell me what's going on between you and Frank. You've been avoiding the topic all weekend," Jana said.

"There's not really that much to tell. It's the same old problem. We're together, and things are going well. Then I just get really bored with him. He's totally neurotic and doesn't want to leave the house, so we wind up hanging out in his apartment watching movies. He doesn't like daylight, so he keeps the shades drawn all day, and it's so macabre. He's just not normal. Then when I can't take it anymore, I pick an argument with him, he gets angry, and we break up. Once we're apart, I'm initially happy and start doing more things with friends. I realize when I have a little distance what a case he is and how I'm wasting my time with him. But then I just get lonely again and wind up calling him. This time, though, I really made him angry, and I'm not sure if we'll ever get back together."

"I think you ought to get out of that relationship while you can."

"Yeah, that's easy for you to say. You already have someone."

"I'm going to ask Michael if he knows anyone we can fix you up with."

"All right, but none of your broomstick-brigade friends."

Repressed, prudish WASPs were what Camille referred to as the "broomstick brigade."

They reminisced about old times when they had worked together, and then they went to bed. On Sunday, they went out for brunch at the Black Pearl by the harbor. They walked along the docks looking at the sailboats and small yachts that were moored there. Camille went into a few shops to buy some souvenirs.

"I wish you could stay longer," Jana said. "There's so much to see. We didn't get a chance to go through any of the Bellevue mansions or to the wildlife preserve at Sachuest Beach."

"I wish I could stay longer too. But Gary will be home, and I've got to get ready for work. Anyway, I came mainly to see you. Next time, we can do more of the sights."

They exchanged bear hugs at the stations and waved goodbye. Jana drove slowly back to Newport thinking about how she missed having her good friend close by. But then again, maybe they wouldn't get along so well if they saw each other so often, she laughed to herself.

At home, she made a pot of tea and curled up on the living room couch with a novel she was reading that took place in southern India, a spot she had always wanted to visit. She pulled an afghan over herself and got comfortable. It was nice to have the house all to herself again. Peaceful. Through the open window, a sea breeze flew in—and with it a memory from childhood. From the time she was eight until she was about sixteen, Jana's parents had taken two weeks at the Jersey Shore each summer. They stayed in a beautiful hotel facing the sea. Each day, they walked along the boardwalk down to the south end of the town to while away the hours on the beach. In the late afternoons, they returned tanned and tired to take naps before dinner. Jana would lie on the bed in her small hotel room and listen to the sound of the ocean as she dropped off to sleep. It was like that now. Exactly like that. She read for a while and drifted off to sleep. When she awoke, it was getting dark, and she was hungry. She prepared a quick salad with some bread and poured herself a glass of wine. In the evening, Jana looked over some new magazines she thought of writing for and dashed off a few query letters.

Her thoughts were drawn to Drew. She wondered how often he thought about her. She decided to make plans to take a trip down to New York City. She wanted to see her cousin Adrienne anyway, maybe her father, if he was around, and perhaps have lunch with Drew.

After spending a few days with Adrienne in New York, Jana made arrangements to meet Drew for lunch. She headed over to Yorkville and the Heidelberg restaurant near Eighty-Sixth and Second Avenue. She felt breathless with anticipation. There he was, sitting at a table waiting for her. He stood up, and they embraced. They made small talk. Jana ordered but was barely focused on what she ate.

"How are things going?" he asked.

Jana spoke animatedly about her life in Newport. "Drew, life is so different in Newport. It's as if I am in another world. The town is wonderful, and I love the new house. I'm busy with the Charleston clip and my writing, but I miss the excitement of the city, and I never thought I would say that. I also miss working with you in Spanish Harlem."

Drew smiled. "It's great to see you, and it sounds like things are going well for you. We've almost finished the last of the houses on the street where you worked with me. How is Michael doing?"

"Michael is doing well. He is still in New Mexico shooting his latest film. He says it's going well. I'm not sure when he'll be home. I flew out to see him, which was a wonderful trip. But it is still lonely sometimes without him home. It's good to get down to the city and see old friends, reconnect with my cousin Adrienne."

"I'm sure."

The two chatted for a while, and then Drew said he would have to run because he was late for a meeting. They embraced and discussed when they might get together again. Drew told Jana to call him when she was coming to the city next time.

CHAPTER 6

———〜〜୦ଵ୧ୠଵ୧ୠ୦ଵ〜〜———

Discoveries

Jana arrived home that evening, and there was a voice mail message from Michael. She called him before even unpacking.

Michael answered immediately. "Hi, darling. I've got some great news. I've decided we all need a break from filming, so I will be flying home in the next day or two for a few weeks!"

"Oh, honey, that is great news. I was just telling Adi when I was in New York how it is lonely without you for these long stretches of time."

"Oh, how was your visit to New York?"

"It was great to see Adrienne, and I wish I could have seen Dad, but he was away again, as usual. When will you be here?"

"I'll call you as soon as I have the flight information, but it should be soon—within the next forty-eight hours."

"OK. I can't wait to see you, honey. Let me know as soon as you can. Love you."

"I will. Love you tons. See you soon. Bye."

———ww•o•ⓒⓝⓞⓒ•ⓝ•o•ww———

Michael hung up the phone and looked around the trailer. He took a long hot shower and stretched out on the bed. Sitting in front of the television, he ate his dinner mindlessly, unable to concentrate on the screen. In an otherwise perfect scenario, the specter of his concealment ruined his reverie of the return home. Almost daily, he was haunted by the knowledge that he would have to share his secret with her. He could not conjure up how she might react, no matter how many times he tried to imagine the various scenarios. But he didn't have to think about it right now, he assured himself. Instead, he lit a cigarette, inhaled deeply, and leaned back on the bed. Quickly, he made a few phone calls to discuss the shooting schedule and managed to watch television for a while. He was glad to find that he was sleepy by ten and turned in for the night.

Jana sped to the Providence airport, as rehearsal had gone longer than expected. She looked forward to spending some time with Michael at home after he completed this movie. She pulled up to the arrival area, and Michael waved as he approached the car.

"Sorry I'm late, honey. Martins was in true form today. Everything had to be repeated again and again until my feet felt numb."

They exchanged a kiss, and Michael folded his hand over hers.

"No worries. I'm just glad to be home."

Back at the house, Jana smiled and announced, "I am going to fix you something special for dinner—one of your favorites: grilled salmon, sweet potatoes, and asparagus."

Michael smiled back at her. "Thank you, honey!"

As they ate, Michael looked around the dining room at all the familiar symbols of home one grows attached to. He had missed being in his own home. He breathed a sigh of relief, got up, and walked over to the window to look at the sea. Though it was nighttime, he could see the curl of white waves and hear the crash of surf hitting the beach. He cracked open the window. Once again, dark thoughts rushed in to haunt him. *Will things be the same once I tell her?* In the kitchen, he poured himself a cup of coffee. Then, sitting in a chair by the living room window, he looked across at Jana. She sat on the couch repairing a hole in the toe of her tights.

"Jana," he began, "there's something I need to talk to you about. I don't know if there will ever be a right time to tell you or how you will feel about it, but …"

"What is it?" Jana asked.

"Many years ago, before I met you, I was working with some friends of David's, the film writer I was having dinner with when we first met. I was actually still a kid, really. We decided to take a trip to Brazil on the spur of the moment to see the carnival and with an idea to maybe film a movie there. I was not really enthusiastic about it because I was in an emotional slump. During the first week, we went out almost every night, enjoying all the sights and sounds, taking pictures of the carnival. I began to feel better and more positive about the trip. A guy traveling with us, Tiago, was from Brazil, and he knew several people in the industry. On one of our evening jaunts, we ran into a group of his friends, who joined us for drinks. There was a Brazilian woman who spoke English, and we began talking. She was a film editor. We became involved. I needed someone desperately then. I wasn't doing any work, and she helped me to come alive again. It only lasted for the few months we were there, and afterward, we wrote a few times. She had a daughter, Andrea, and I am her father. She is fifteen now. And Claudia, her mother, is coming to the States with Andrea for a pleasure trip. Apparently, Andrea wants to meet me. I always sent money regularly, but it didn't really occur to me that she would want to meet me. I thought about her over the years, but I was young when it happened, and Claudia is married now and has other children, so I just assumed Andrea would think of her stepfather as her father."

Jana stared at Michael. "It's not the news, Michael. I just don't understand why you waited until now to tell me. You could have told me this a long time ago. I probably would have accepted it better. No, I *know* I would have accepted it better if you'd told me sooner. Would you have even told me at all if it weren't for the fact that your 'daughter' wants to meet you?"

"I wanted to tell you many times, Jana. When we first moved to Newport, I almost did. But I was afraid it might ruin what we have. I was afraid you might get upset and angry, especially since we'd talked about the possibility of having children of our own. I knew at those times that I was pretending I didn't have a child when I did. After we decided not to have children, I felt even guiltier. I'm so sorry, Jana. I didn't mean to wait so long before sharing this news with you."

"But you did. You wrote to this woman regularly. You sent money to a daughter I did not even know you had, without any reservation about keeping it from me. I can't talk about this anymore right now, Michael!" Jana angrily threw her sewing across the room, walked off, and slammed the bedroom door behind her.

Sometime later, Jana emerged from their bedroom, having changed into her nightclothes, her face blotchy. Michael looked up nervously to see the expression on her face.

Jana said, "So now what? You know, of course, that it does change things for us, Michael. You have a daughter who wants to meet you, another significant person in your life now."

"I know. I just hope you know that there has never been anyone like you in my life and there never will be."

"I know. What are you going to do now? Are you going to meet her?"

"Well, they are flying into Los Angeles and staying with friends in San Diego. So I was thinking that when I go back to finish things up in Santa Fe, I could fly out to my parents, stay with them, and meet her then."

"I suppose that could work. How do you feel about meeting her?"

"Just knowing that I have a child is a lot different from actually meeting her. I'm not sure how I feel—flattered, nervous."

"Maybe she is just curious to see what you're like and that will be that."

"I thought about that. I guess I'll just have to wait and see what happens."

"I'm exhausted. Let's go to bed," Jana said.

"Yes, it's been a very long day," Michael said.

They lay in bed using the changing screen of the television as a background for their thoughts. Michael felt relief that Jana had accepted the news better than he'd expected. Now his thoughts turned toward the prospect of meeting his child for the first time. Jana thought about how true it was that no matter how well you think you know someone, there is always another layer completely obscured. She thought, too, about how Michael was not the only one with secrets.

The next week flew by for Jana. Having Michael at home was wonderful. They got together with friends, and Jana felt as she had when they first started living together. She was a bit anxious about Michael's news, but overall, she was content and secure. Michael stayed home and made dinner while Jana was out at rehearsal most days. After dinner, they went for a ride around the ten miles of the famous Ocean Drive with its historic landmarks and stunning coastal views. Other nights, they took in a movie or went for a long walk.

On Monday, Jana arrived at Rosecliff for rehearsal on the Charleston clip. Throughout the day, she didn't feel well and couldn't wait to get home and lie down. Before she had a chance, however, she deposited the day's lunch into the toilet. She crawled under the covers and comforted herself, with nothing to do but rest. Jana soon fell asleep to the quiet sound of late afternoon, of seagulls and waves against the shoreline. She dreamed she was in a dance class practicing with other children for a ballet recital. She couldn't get the steps quite right. The teacher frowned. Jana tried harder. She couldn't get it. *Oh my God*, she thought. Now the other children were watching, staring, pointing. She heard a noise coming from somewhere in the room, like a siren, a shrill whistling—a fire drill? Jana woke up and realized the phone was ringing.

"Hello?"

"Oh, hi. Jana?"

"Yes?"

"This is Leah. Did I wake you?"

"Oh, Leah, it's so good to hear from you! No, that's OK. I was just resting. How are you?"

"I'm fine, thanks. I'm calling because I'm going to be working in Rhode Island for a few months with the RI State Ballet on a special project and wanted to let you know."

"Oh, that's great. When are you starting, and where are you staying?"

"I've rented an apartment in Providence not far from the State Ballet. I know there will be long hours, so I wanted to be close. I've even brought my parrot, Lolita, with me for company and well, to be honest, there isn't anyone willing to take care of her," she laughed. "I was wondering if you could get away one evening for dinner."

"Sure. When were you thinking?"

"How about next week? After I'm settled, I'll give you a call."

"OK, great. Talk to you then."

Jana fell back on the pillow and lay thinking about Leah and the State Ballet. She'd taught some classes there and had fond memories. It was great to have a new friend like Leah. She was one of those women you thought you'd enjoy getting to know well but thought it probably wouldn't happen.

"How are you feeling, hon?" Michael said, interrupting her thoughts.

"Better, thanks, but not hungry. Can you fix yourself something?"

"Sure. I have some ideas for a new project, so I'll be working in the den if you need me."

"OK." Jana rolled over and tried to fall asleep but instead became dimly aware that she was feeling unhappy about her life. She couldn't pinpoint it. It wasn't the news about Michael's daughter, although that had been unsettling. This went deeper. In fact, it had nothing to do with Michael. It was that her life was just not what she wanted it to be. She had been thinking about babies since Michael announced he was a father. But that wasn't really it either. She had made peace with not having children. It had been her choice, freely made, and while occasionally she had pangs of motherhood envy, she was happy with her decision.

In the evening, a late-spring storm arrived, blowing the curtains and capsizing ornaments on the windowsill. Michael rose to close the window and noticed the ocean churning in the wind. He wondered what it would be like to meet Andrea for the first time. What would he say to her? How should he be with her? The plan was for Claudia to contact him when she arrived in San Diego, and they would make arrangements to meet. He tried to work for a while, but as the storm intensified, so did his thoughts of the future. Soon he would be in between projects. He enjoyed the break, yet he was restless when not working. There were a few things in the fire but nothing substantial. He would have to wait and see what unfolded.

———∿∿∘◦◯◦∘∿∿———

The following week, Jana made arrangements with Leah to meet at Christie's for dinner. Leah was already seated at a table when Jana arrived. Leah waved and gave a bright smile. She looked stunning in a sleeveless peach dress and with her hair twisted up.

"I see you found the place. Any problem getting here?" Jana asked.

"No, your directions were perfect."

They ordered, and Jana said, "So tell me about the project you're working on with the RI State Ballet."

"Oh, it's very exciting. A friend and I were asked to choreograph a piece that will be included in their upcoming annual recital. The dancers are wonderful to work with since they are all professionals and very talented. I feel lucky to be a part of this work. We began rehearsal this week, and it's been basically getting acquainted. I anticipate it will be about two months of rehearsal before production. You'll have to come and see it! I could have commuted from where I live in Massachusetts, but I wanted to be more hands-on and thought it would be fun to spend some time in Rhode Island."

"I think it's a great idea. Do you have any other friends in this area?"

"Yes, my friend Paul, who's working on the project with me, is also staying in Providence. He was the one who suggested I rent a place. And I know people from the company. We go out. It's nice."

"I worked for the company last summer for a few months. With the Larsdens. Do you know them? They are retired now."

"The name is familiar," Leah answered.

Over dinner, Jana and Leah chatted about acquaintances they had in common. They laughed about the trials and triumphs of rehearsing. Jana recalled how Mr. Larsden used to make jokes about the ineptness of a couple doing a pas de deux. Jana was struck by Leah's easy manner and graceful way.

It was almost ten when they finally parted. Jana invited Leah to come to dinner and meet Michael later in the week before he returned to New Mexico. In the morning, Jana got up early and did some work on an article before going to rehearsal. She liked the early mornings because the town was still sleeping and nothing interrupted her thoughts. She was able to accomplish twice as much as at any other time.

At Rosecliff, Jana waited with the other dancers for the choreographer. They stood around talking about the scene and the fact that it was almost finished. In fact, Martins had said that they might be able to wrap up that day.

"We'll have to celebrate!" Julie exclaimed.

"Definitely," Wendy chimed in. "Let's spend the evening at the Red Parrot eating all the desserts we haven't been able to eat the last few months!"

"I'm there," Gwen said.

"It looks like he's ready for us," Jana said.

The dancers moved into position. Martins began taking them through the routine. Jana loved the music, which was always uplifting. Everyone seemed to be on today, and after a few run-throughs, they were ready to shoot. After a successful shoot, everyone was always relieved. That part of the rehearsal was behind them, and they could relax. It resulted in a break of about fifteen to twenty minutes. The women milled around laughing and talking. They stood out on the back balcony of the mansion looking out at the carefully manicured lawn, which stretched down to the sea. It was warming up, and they drifted out onto the steps, where they sat toweling off their necks and faces and adjusting their hair. Some sipped cold water from plastic cups.

"I can't believe we finally wrapped up that whole segment today!"

"Yeah, it really was a shock. Maybe even Martins is getting tired," Wendy said.

"I don't know. Personally, I think he's bionic," Julie added.

"He does seem tireless," Jana said.

"I hope he's not gonna keep us too long today. I have things to do," Julie said.

"You say that every day, Julie," the others said in unison.

"Yeah, and every day I mean it. Just because we made the Charleston cut doesn't mean Martins has control over our lives. I mean, it's not my fault he doesn't have a life."

"Shush, here he comes!"

Martins came out onto the patio clapping his hands,

and the women reluctantly filed back inside. They ran over the last bit of the scene, and Martins announced it was a wrap and thanked them all for their hard work. Joyfully, the women hurriedly changed and headed out to the Red Parrot on Thames Street to celebrate. They found a booth in the back and ordered drinks and appetizers. They toasted to having survived Martins, the strict taskmaster.

Later on, at home, the phone rang, and it was Camille.

"Hey, Jana, what's going on?"

"Not much. What about you?

"Well, Frank and I are back together. I guess we're just fated to be together."

"You mean you're too lazy to bother looking for someone more appropriate."

"Yeah, that too. Anyway, for the moment, things are going well. How's rehearsal?"

"Oh, we finished up today! Finally. I can't believe it's really over. We all went out to celebrate. It's kind of bittersweet. I will miss those women. Also, Michael's daughter is coming to California with her mother. Wants to meet her father."

"You're kidding! How do you feel about that?"

"Well, I already told you the story, right?"

"Yes, but you didn't say anything about their coming to the States."

"I'm not sure how I feel. Still mulling it over, though there's not much I can do about it. Of course he wants to meet her."

They chatted for a while, catching up. Then Michael came to the doorway and motioned to Jana that he wanted to talk to her. She hung up and came out into the living room.

"I miss you, honey. I haven't seen you all day," Michael remarked.

"I'm sorry. I miss you too. How was your day?"

"Good. It looks like I'll probably be going back west next week and meeting Andrea the following weekend. I should be able to finish up in New Mexico in a few weeks."

"Great. Well, I invited Leah for dinner Friday evening. I hope that's okay. I want you to meet her."

"No, that's fine. I'd like to meet her."

Jana arrived home early on Friday, having finished up her work at the library. Rosa had already been to clean and Jana enjoyed the satisfaction of putting the finishing touches on the house, straightening and adjusting little things. She set the dining room table and put out the good wineglasses. She selected a special dinnerware pattern. Then she took a long relaxing shower and rested before Michael came home. When Michael arrived, he noticed the care with which the dining room table had been set.

"She must be somebody pretty special," he laughed.

"She is, and I want everything to be just right. I want her to feel comfortable at our place."

"Oh, I'm sure she will, honey. But why is it so important to you?"

"I don't know. I guess I just really value Leah's friendship, and maybe I do want to impress her a little."

When the doorbell rang, it was still light out, as the days were getting longer. Michael went to the door, as Jana was still rushing around with last-minute dinner preparations.

"Hi! You must be Leah. I'm Michael. Come in."

Jana rushed from the kitchen to greet her friend. They embraced, and Jana brought Leah into the living room.

"I'm so glad you're here. You look wonderful, as always. Michael will entertain you for a bit. I'm almost finished in the kitchen."

"Oh, that's fine—don't hurry on my account. I'm fine. I'm looking forward to a little tête-à-tête with this guy of yours."

Leah sat in one of their oversized chairs and Michael on the couch nearby.

"I want to thank you for taking Jana around Santa Fe, showing her the sights. She still talks about what a great time you two had together."

"Oh, she was great company for me too. My brother gets tired of my dragging him around to places when I'm there. You have such a beautiful home here; the view of the ocean is spectacular."

"Thanks, yes, we were lucky to find this place. It is peaceful to come home to after being away working."

They chatted about Michael's latest film and Leah's current project with the ballet company, and Jana announced that dinner was ready. Jana had prepared broiled steak, baked potatoes, and salad. There was lemon sherbet for dessert. The meal was pronounced a gustatory success, and they carried their wineglasses to the living room. Leah told Jana and Michael about herself: her life in Massachusetts as a dance instructor, her failed marriage to a choreographer, and the passing of all her family except for her older brother in Santa Fe. Jana observed that despite adversity, Leah was able to maintain a carefree, happy attitude toward life. She wondered what her secret was. Michael and Leah seemed to get along well. Leah laughed at Michael's sense of humor and engaging manner. Jana was pleased that the evening had gone well. It grew late, and Leah thanked them and said good night.

"I can see why you like her," Michael commented afterward. "She's so full of life, so upbeat."

"Isn't she? And we have a great deal in common, so it's nice to have someone like her around."

"You did a great job, darling, with everything."

"Thanks. Come on. Let's go to bed. We can clean up in the morning."

CHAPTER 7

Shooting from the Heart

J ana gave Michael an extra squeeze at the airport before he boarded his plane. She hated these moments when they were separated, but eventually she enjoyed the time on her own.

Driving toward Newport, Jana admired how everything was now in full bloom. The sky was clear blue, which was rare this close to the ocean. Even the air smelled sweet. Summer took a long time to make its presence fully known in Newport. Waiting for the weather to warm up was agonizing. The aroma of sweet rose hips along Sachuest Beach in Middletown filled her lungs as she drove past the shimmering ocean in the early-morning sun. The sea oats were tall and wafted in the breeze. On impulse, Jana drove down to Sachuest Wildlife Preserve. The preserve had different trails, and Jana especially liked one that ran along the ocean. As she walked, a rabbit scurried across the path, and various colorful birds flitted around. She wondered what other creatures lay hiding from sight in the depth of the bushes and trees. Way in the distance, Jana once saw a deer. She wished she had brought her binoculars so she could enjoy looking out to sea and watching the freighters on the horizon. Seagulls perched on the rocks and squawked overhead. A foghorn droned in the distance. Wildflowers sprung up everywhere, and she picked some to take home. The trail was good physical and mental exercise, and she tried to go once every few months, except during the winter.

A bit later, from a nearby coffee shop, she telephoned Leah. "Hi! It's Jana. What are you up to?"

"Hi! Not much. Where are you?"

"I just took a drive down to Sachuest Wildlife Preserve and back. Feel like driving down to meet for a drink?"

"Sure. I was just thinking how beautiful Newport must be today. That sounds nice. How about in an hour?"

"Great. Do you know the Black Pearl?"

"Yes, I think so. Bowen's Wharf, right?"

"Yes, that's right. I'll meet you there in an hour."

"Good. See you then. Bye."

Jana smiled thinking what excellent company Leah was. Despite her nasty divorce, she seemed self-assured and contented. She was always good-humored and funny. With Michael away again, Jana was especially appreciative of their friendship. Jana pulled up at a parking meter near the restaurant. She was a little early but went in and ordered a glass of merlot. Looking out over the harbor, she could see the sailboats and yachts bobbing in the ripples of waves. Just then, Leah came breezing in, glowing and smiling broadly.

"Hi! What a great day, huh?" she exclaimed. "The traffic driving from Providence was light, so I made it in record time."

After a couple of drinks, the two women found themselves laughing over the idiosyncrasies of dance teachers. The wine began to relax Jana, and she considered confiding her interest in Drew. Until now, she had told one other person, and that was Camille. As Jana had hoped, Leah had a nonjudgmental and compassionate response to her story. As they talked, the two ordered a light supper, as Jana didn't like cooking for one and Leah hated cooking.

"How fascinating that you and this man's paths crossed the way they did," Leah remarked.

"Yes, and that he has treated me in such a special way. I have developed these feelings for him, Leah, and it's like nothing I've ever felt before. It's like seeing the Taj Mahal and thinking what a wonderful place to own and then, suddenly … it's yours. He is the most beautiful person, within and without, that I've ever known."

"I can't even imagine. But what are you going to do? I mean, if it were to become serious? Could that even happen?"

"I really don't know. I just cherish the times I get to see him for now. Nothing may ever happen. But I want to go down to New York soon to see him again. I long to see him."

After dinner, Jana invited Leah back to the house for coffee. "I hate the thought of going back to that big empty house," Jana confessed. Leah followed her back to the house on Ocean Drive. Inside, the rooms had grown damp, and Jana lit a fire. The two women curled up with afghans and chatted until Leah tired and left for the drive home.

A week later, Jana managed to make plans to meet Drew in New York. It was a mild spring evening, and Drew had selected a restaurant near Jana's old stomping grounds when she had lived in the city. Jana had noticed Drew no longer wore his priest collar when they met. Then again, he rarely wore it any longer except on formal occasions. When Jana walked in, she noticed that his hair was combed back, and he wore a light blue shirt that matched his eyes. Drew had ordered a manhattan and was smoking a cigarette when Jana arrived. He stood up to greet her, and they embraced. After ordering, they caught up with each other's news while waiting for their food. Jana was mesmerized by Drew's presence, his charisma. She confessed to herself that he had a way of making her hands shake, as well as making her feel like she and Drew were the only ones in the restaurant. After they finished their meal, and a few drinks later, Drew asked her a question—a question she had hoped for, longed for, and waited for since meeting him that first time.

"Did it ever occur to you that it might be difficult for me not to make a pass at you?"

Jana lowered her glass. Sitting there stunned, she asked, "Could you please repeat the question?"

Of course it had occurred to her. In fact, she had imagined it many times. She thought she was crazy for wanting Drew, for thinking he ever could or would want her, that she was truly … shooting from the heart.

But there it was. Seconds went by as the question hung in the air.

"Uh, I never really thought about it before," she managed to say. For she did not want Drew to know that she had even contemplated it. The conversation that was normally filled with underlying tension relaxed now as they looked at each other and smiled. Drew lit another cigarette and exhaled slowly. The conversation turned quickly to where they could meet, how they could arrange to be together. Jana had to consider when Michael would be away again, who she could tell him she was visiting *this time*. All the way home, back to Newport, Jana could think only of seeing Drew again.

When Jana awoke the next morning, she realized in a rush the events of the day before. Perhaps the vague stirrings of discontent had been leading up to this moment with Drew all along. For the first time in a long while, she felt content. The phone rang, and Jana dreaded it would be Michael. She let it ring, deciding to shower first and then call back.

"Michael?"

"Hi, honey. I tried to call you a few minutes ago."

"Oh, I was in the shower. How are things going?"

"Okay. I should be finished by the end of the week and then off to San Diego."

"Are you nervous about meeting Andrea?"

"Yes, but I'm trying to stay composed for now. Work is keeping me busy. I just wanted to let you know I'm settled in and already missing you. What are you up to today?"

"I've got to finish an article I promised for Penny. That's about all."

"You sound very serious, honey. Everything all right?"

"Oh, yeah. Just a lot of writing ahead of me."

"Okay, I'll let you go. Miss you."

"I miss you too."

"I'll call you later this evening."

"OK, talk to you later. Bye."

CHAPTER 8

—◦◦◦◦◦◦◦◦◦—

San Diego

Michael swallowed a couple of Tums. He was beginning to experience that familiar knot in his stomach that always preceded an anxiety-provoking event. Shortly, he would be having dinner with some of his coworkers to celebrate wrapping up filming, finishing the last bit of editing, and watching a first screening. Instead of feeling celebratory, Michael was focused on meeting his daughter. He would see Andrea, in a matter of days, for the first time. He was filled with both anticipation and dread.

Once in the restaurant, however, after a few drinks, he embraced the mood of his coworkers. After dinner, they retired to the screening room to watch the run-through. There was applause and much back slapping as the credits rolled—Michael Wagner, Director—and Michael allowed himself to experience that sweet satisfaction of having accomplished something worthwhile. He excused himself then, feigning fatigue, to return to the hotel and rest before his flight to San Diego in the morning to see his parents.

During the flight, Michael's thoughts drifted to possible scenarios of his meeting with Andrea. Would she be tentative or scrutinizing? Would she embrace him warmly? And what would Claudia's reaction be? After all, from what he could gather, the meeting was Andrea's idea and not her mother's. Before he realized it, they were landing, and Michael's mother was waving as he came into the waiting area.

"Darling," she said and smiled, hugging him. "I'm so glad you're finally here. Your father and I were just saying that it's been too long this time between visits." Michael was the only child of the Wagners, and they tended to dote on him. He'd had a younger brother by three years who was killed in a freak paragliding accident off the cliffs of La Jolla. They'd never gotten over this tragedy. Tim had been eighteen at the time and would have been in his thirties now.

"Congratulations, son, on what will be an Academy Award nomination, I'm sure!"

"Dad, you say that every time I finish a film. And every time you are so far off," Michael replied jokingly. "I'll just be glad if we break even with this one. We went way over budget. And some good reviews would be nice. Anyway, it's good to be here too."

They drove to a little Mexican place in La Jolla for lunch. Afterward, they went for a short drive by the ocean. Julia and Josh Wagner were good parents, although a bit overprotective ever since losing Tim. Julia was a retired high school teacher and Josh a banker. Julia presented all sorts of possible excursions for the rest of the day, but Michael just wanted to get to their place and get settled. His parents had a comfortable three-bedroom condominium in San Diego proper. There was a small balcony with a view of the ocean.

Once they were back at the apartment, Julia asked, "When are you meeting Andrea? Do you need anything? Is it cool enough in here for you?"

"Mom," Michael replied, "you and Jana have the same habit of asking me a string of questions without waiting for an answer."

"Oh, sorry," Julia replied.

"I'm meeting her tomorrow for lunch, and everything is fine. You don't need to fuss over me so." He leaned over and kissed her lightly on the cheek.

They sat around the kitchen table that evening catching up until around midnight. Michael talked about Jana's latest endeavors, their difficulties at times dealing with being separated when he was working, and their life in Newport. His parents promised that they would seriously consider a trip during the summer to spend some time with Michael and Jana. They were not keen on traveling and couldn't take the weather when it was cold and damp. He caught up on all their events and the gossip that parents of this age somehow feel is important for their children to keep abreast of.

Michael lay in bed for a long time listening to the loud ticking clock his mother seemed to feel was a reassuring and lulling sound. It seemed like such a long time ago when he had fallen in love with Claudia. Now, he was to meet the product of their passionate and impulsive union in Andrea. Although he'd seen pictures of her, it was still difficult to conjure up a live human being, a Brazilian teenager who was his daughter, his offspring. Very soon, however, it would be quite real, and all the unknowns filled his mind. He drifted off eventually and woke in good spirits early in the morning. Jana telephoned him to wish him luck, and he promised to call her that night to let her know how things had gone.

He took the phone number Claudia had given him out of his wallet and punched in the numbers. After a few rings, he heard the familiar "Oi."

"Oi," Michael responded.

"Como voce esta? Oh, Michael, hi. How are you? We were waiting for your call." They spoke for a few minutes confirming the time and place of their meeting.

Michael drove slowly to his destination. He swallowed a few more Tums and wondered how he would be able to eat anything at this point. What if she hated him? What if she had been waiting to tell him what a rotten father he had been all her life? He had to admit he felt guilty just sending a monthly check and never bothering to visit or send for her to come to the United States. Perhaps she considered her stepfather to be her real father and merely had a curiosity to meet him.

The day was sunny and warm, with a wonderful breeze coming off the ocean. Michael took a deep breath and tried to relax and enjoy the surroundings. One way or another, it would soon be over, and he could go back to his comfortable life. He approached the rendezvous point. He could see two women standing near an awning at the corner, chatting and laughing. He craned his neck to get a better look as he slowly drove by trying to find parking. One of the women looked to be in her forties, with dark hair and generous makeup, and she wore a red blouse and a long black skirt that stirred in the breeze. She wore those sexy sandals that have lots of thin straps, black patent leather, crisscrossing her feet. She threw back her head laughing, and Michael knew it was Claudia. The other woman was much younger, tall and slender with long black hair cascading down her back; a sleeveless white top; and a long, flowing transparent pinkish skirt. She, too, wore sandals. Michael could feel his heart pumping as he parked the car and stepped out. The two women suddenly stopped their laughter and looked at him as he crossed the street toward them. Then Claudia waved, walked toward him, and embraced him warmly.

"Este e seu pai, Andrea," Claudia said, holding Michael's arm and smiling. Michael could see tears welling up in Claudia's eyes. Andrea leaned over and tentatively gave her father a hug. The two smiled at each other. He took a long look at her. She was more beautiful than he could have imagined. She had her mother's coloring, a young girlish figure, and a lovely sculptured face. A wide smile revealed perfect teeth. Deep brown eyes stared back at him. They walked together into the restaurant to a table Michael had reserved. It had a Brazilian flavor to it, which Michael had specifically chosen. It was a quiet, cheery place. Michael sat between his ex-lover and his daughter. At first, they exchanged small talk while waiting for their drinks to arrive. Then Michael was suddenly filled with questions for Andrea—about her school, social life, boyfriends, and lifestyle in Brazil. He had forgotten the enthusiasm for life so many Brazilians have and the passion with which they described events. Both women laughed often. Claudia occasionally touched his arm, which gave him a comforting feeling that things were going well. Michael asked about Armani, Claudia's husband, and how their business was going. Claudia had been fortunate enough to marry a fairly wealthy businessman and was able to travel often and not want for anything material.

Michael was struck by Andrea's sophistication and poise. Though only sixteen, she could have been a twenty-two-year-old American girl. As he watched her expressive gestures, he began to relax and enjoy her. She did not appear to be in the least upset with him and actually appeared rather matter of fact about the circumstances of her life. Andrea was very close to her stepfather and to her mother. Claudia had written Michael over the years that theirs was a close-knit family and all got along well. After marrying Armani, Claudia had two more children, a boy and another girl. They were eleven and thirteen. Around the table, they exchanged pictures of Claudia's children and husband and of Michael and Jana. Andrea gave Michael a recent picture of herself. Claudia had decided to come to California to visit friends and because Andrea was thinking of going to college in the US. She would be ready for college in two years, and they'd decided to drive around to a few campuses in California. They were also taking a tour of the coast with their Brazilian friends. Claudia admitted to Michael that it would be hard to allow Andrea to come to the US for school, as she would miss her terribly. She preferred that she attend university in Brazil. Michael replied that if Andrea decided to attend school in the US, she would have a second home in Newport to come to whenever she wanted.

Michael chatted about his film work and his life with Jana. Andrea plied him with questions about his work and life in the US.

"What kind of films do you make, Michael?" Andrea asked her father.

They continued the conversation over coffee and decided to take a drive down to one of the nearby beaches.

It was Sunday, and the beach was packed with surfers, bathers, and sun worshippers, as well as people playing Frisbee and volleyball. Older people sat farther back under umbrellas, chatting and people watching. Claudia and Andrea slipped off their sandals and walked alongside Michael. The waves lapped at their feet. After a while, Andrea fell behind collecting shells while her father and mother walked ahead.

"What a beautiful daughter we have," Michael exclaimed. "And what a wonderful job you have done raising her!"

"Oh, thank you, Michael, but I cannot take all the credit. Armani has been a strong, positive influence in her life."

They began to reminisce about their time together in Brazil and of the passion they'd shared for each other. They walked arm in arm as they talked.

"Do you ever have any regrets about us?" Michael asked.

"I think timing is everything as I grow older," Claudia replied. "And sometimes there are incredibly wonderful people that we only get to love for a short period of time. I try not to look back."

"We are both happy now, and I guess that's what's important," Michael said. They spoke about the money Michael had sent over the years and how Claudia had kept telling Michael he did not need to send any, as Armani was a good provider to all the children. But Michael felt that this was his duty and the least he could do until Andrea finished college and was an adult. Eventually, they turned back and caught up with their daughter, who showed them her collection of American seashells.

On the ride back into town, they fell silent, all in their own worlds of thoughts. Michael thought about the years of his daughter's youth he had missed and the years to come that he might miss as well. But perhaps not; time would tell. He wondered what Claudia thought about seeing Michael again and his finally meeting Andrea. And what it was like for Andrea to see her parents in the front seat together. The only father she had ever known was Armani. Michael escorted them to their car and gave Claudia a hug.

"Cuide bem de voce, Michael," Claudia whispered to him.

"I will. You too," Michael replied. Then he embraced Andrea. "You are growing into a beautiful young woman, and I am so proud of you." The tears came into his eyes despite his attempt at delaying them.

"Obrigado, and I am happy to finally meet you," Andrea said.

Claudia promised to let him know when they would come for a visit again. In the car, Michael let the tears flow freely. It was not just the emotion of meeting his daughter but also the relief that it had gone well and he had gotten through it. He had a beautiful, intelligent daughter, and things seemed to have worked out for the best. He was grateful for that. He couldn't wait to get back and call Jana to let her know how well things had gone.

CHAPTER 9

—⁓∿⦿⦿⦿⦿⦿∿⁓—

The Center

They met at Grand Central Terminal by the clock at the information booth. Drew had chosen the place. As Jana approached, sunlight shone in glowing squares through the large panels of windows above. They found each other quickly at the appointed time, and Drew ushered her across the street into a large restaurant, where they ordered breakfast. Jana was filled with anticipation yet nervousness. She sat quietly eating and thinking about what was to come.

The quiet of the restaurant made it more awkward until Drew commented, "I wish someone would break a plate."

Neither said much. The restaurant led through to the lobby of a hotel, where Jana and Drew took the elevator to the eighth floor. Jana experienced a slight feeling of trepidation, of expectations that might be dashed. They entered the room, which had twin beds.

"Do you want to take a shower together?" Drew asked.

"No, that's okay. You go ahead, and I'll wait for you," she replied.

Jana lay on the bed looking out the window while listening to the water run. When Drew emerged, Jana was filled with excitement and disbelief that this moment had actually arrived. She was about to make love with a monsignor. But to her, he was just Drew. After waiting for so long, being in love for so long, the feeling was exquisite—a combination of passion and expressed love for each other. The moment their bodies touched and she felt him on top of her, entering her, was the culmination of everything she had wished for. A feeling of ecstasy flooded her body. They lay together on the twin bed, stealing some time together. Time where Drew should have been somewhere else, definitely not here, holding Jana.

"When will we see each other again?" Jana asked softly.

"I'm not sure. I have several obligations over the next few months. But I do have some good news for you. I'm scheduled to come and speak at the University of Rhode Island in a few weeks. I might be able to work out a visit if you know someplace we could meet."

"Oh, Drew, that is such great news! I can definitely find somewhere either in Kingston or Newport. Give me the dates, and I'll let you know."

They dressed hurriedly now and departed the hotel. Jana took a cab to Penn Station, and Drew was off to parts unknown.

—⟡⟡⟡⟡⟡—

It was a warm, sunny afternoon with a light breeze. Michael and Jana sat outside sipping drinks on the porch and looking out over the ocean. Jana was happy for Michael's return. She wondered, however, if there were other secrets he hadn't told her. Then, too, her feelings for Drew widened the distance between Michael and her.

"I couldn't have asked for things to go better," Michael began. "Claudia made me feel so at ease. Andrea is growing into a beautiful young woman. She looks like her mother more and more." Michael showed Jana a picture of Andrea.

"She is beautiful. How did she respond to you?"

"Oh, Jana, she was wonderful. Pleasant and talkative, as if we'd always been friends. There was no animosity or sense of distance from her. I felt very comfortable. I asked her about her life in Brazil, and she asked about my directing and about you."

"About me?"

"Yes, I showed her a picture, and she asked all about you."

"Hmm, and what did you tell her?"

"I told her about what you do and how lucky I am to have found you." Michael smiled. Jana leaned over and kissed him then.

"We walked on the beach for a while and then went for coffee later and talked some more. I was so impressed by how well she has turned out and told Claudia what a wonderful job she had done."

"How was it at your parents'?"

"Oh, fine. They'll never change. But they miss *you*! I think they're really serious about making a trip out here sometime soon. I'd love for them to see our place. Dad is still under the delusion that I will be nominated for an Academy Award."

"I would love to see them as well," Jana replied.

"Anyway, what have you been up to?"

Jana seized the moment. "Actually, Leah has an idea to start a center utilizing dance, massage, and meditation as therapy for stress relief."

"Sounds great!" Michael replied. "Can I be her first client?"

"How about being my first client?"

"What do you mean?"

"Well, she has asked me to go in with her, as a partner."

Michael sat forward in his chair. "Is that something you really want to do?"

"Yes, I've been giving it a lot of thought, and I think it could be wonderful, combining our knowledge of dance and movement with massage therapy and meditation. I think the time is right for it. It would be a great opportunity and personally very satisfying. I think it could be profitable as well. More profitable than the things I am doing now."

"It does sound like something you'd be good at and enjoy, but what kind of start-up money is involved in a project like this? Where would you set it up?"

"Leah is working on getting an idea of how much money we would need. We're thinking of doing something maybe in Providence. I would like to have her over for dinner so we could talk about it together. She has much more of an understanding of the business aspects of this kind of venture than I do. Her family used to run a small business."

"Honey, I'm willing to support you in any way I can. You know that. What about the time involved, though? Starting a business can be extraordinarily time consuming."

"I guess in the beginning it could be hectic with long hours, but after a while, I can envision a normal daily routine with weekends for us … when you're here."

Michael put his arm around Jana. "A new phase of your life, huh, kiddo?" He smiled.

Jana smiled back. It was a phase that would prove to be a turning point in their lives beyond what either could imagine right now.

The afternoon was waning, and the two retreated into the house. Michael was pleased to see the flowers Jana had thoughtfully ordered for around the house. He showered and took a nap while Jana prepared dinner. By evening, they sat curled up on the couch reading and enjoying each other's company. It was good to be home, Michael thought, and he breathed in deeply the summer-night sea air as they grew drowsy in the softly lit living room. He was filled with contentment and gratitude for the life he and Jana shared. She seemed to have accepted the reality of his daughter's presence, and he felt a sense of peace about his life.

Over the next several weeks, they made a few weekend jaunts together, and Michael caught up with his medical and financial appointments. They had a few guests visit whom the couple had not seen in months. Michael worked in the backyard supervising the construction of their deck while Jana planted flower gardens. They rearranged furniture and hired people to come in and do a thorough spring-cleaning, including all the windows, after a long musty winter of being shut indoors. Even the weather cooperated with a spate of sunny, warm low-humidity days, which helped to dry out the ever-present dampness of papers, books, and clothes.

Leah came to dinner and captured Michael's interest in the center project. "I'd like to have a target starting date of late fall," Leah began. "That's assuming everything goes as planned."

"That would work well for us," Michael responded. "I probably won't be starting my next film project until fall."

Leah described in detail what she envisioned for the center, her green eyes bright with enthusiasm. Jana sat watching her and found her fervor contagious. She could tell that Michael, too, was impressed not only with the concept but also with how well Leah had thought things through. What Jana could not anticipate was the amount of work that lay ahead for such a project to be successful.

One morning, while Michael was sitting on the porch drinking coffee in his favorite wicker chair, Leah pulled up in her Saab and walked briskly toward him. She was full of smiles, waving happily at him and practically dancing in the front door. Finding Jana in the kitchen, she announced that she'd found the perfect spot for the center. She wanted Jana to come with her right away to see what she thought. Jana hurriedly dressed, and the two were out the door and driving off, waving and shouting to Michael that they had a prospective place. The two women parked along one of main streets of downtown Barrington. It was a Sunday morning, and there wasn't much traffic. Leah inserted the key into the lock and opened the front door. Jana peered inside to see a good-sized front room. Before she could say a word, Leah grabbed her hand and pulled her through the entry into the back rooms. There were about four or five small examining rooms that had been used by the previous renter, a dermatologist who had retired. There were two or three large closets. Several windows permitted lots of light and air.

"Isn't it wonderful?" Leah turned and smiled at Jana. "The location is incredibly good. We're on the main drag, and Barrington is so close to Providence—we couldn't ask for a better spot for the center."

Jana had to admit she was impressed. "But how can we afford the rent in such a great location?"

"It's really quite affordable. The building owner loves the concept of having the center here and is willing to give us a break at least for the first year. So what do you think?"

"I think you are pretty amazing!" Jana replied and gave Leah a hug.

"You like it, then?"

"I think it's wonderful; it completely meets our needs. How soon can we move in?"

"If we want it, it's ours, and we can move in anytime. It's completely ready for occupancy. I met with the owner yesterday."

They began in earnest that week. Michael helped them haul boxes of supplies they had been collecting. They shopped for equipment and ordered what they could not find in stores. They found themselves caught up in the excitement of their new venture. As the weeks drew on, the center began to take shape. The women still had to think of a name for their place, and there were business aspects with which they had to become acquainted. Leah spent time on the phone with her brother in Santa Fe going over and learning about the business of running their place. He had been the primary one involved in the family business in Massachusetts before Leah's parents died. Jana concentrated on decorating and organizing the office into a functional and attractive setting.

One evening, after a month into setting up, the women sat at a little round metal table in the front room with a bottle of wine, flowers in a vase, and a take-out spaghetti dinner.

"Well, Jana, this is our baby. What shall we call it? You're good at names, so let's hear what you've got in mind."

"I think we should go with alliteration. It makes it easier to remember. Something like Barrington Beginnings or the Barrington Balance Center. After all, we're working toward gaining an overall balance for women, aren't we?"

"Barrington Balance Center it is—the BBC!" Leah exclaimed. "I like it. Underneath, we'll say something about stress relief through meditation, massage, and dance."

Over this intimate dinner, and with classical music as accompaniment, they celebrated their new digs and continued to plan for their future as business partners.

In the meantime, Jana had been looking into possibilities for where she and Drew might meet when he came to speak at the University of Rhode Island. Although Drew would stay on campus overnight, Jana made arrangements to pick him up the next day and go to Newport, a twenty-minute drive where they could spend a few hours at a friend's bed-and-breakfast near Bowen's Wharf.

She told Michael she was meeting with the Larsdens, who taught ballet at the university and were interested in learning more about the center. They would have lunch on campus. Although Jana felt guilty for lying to Michael, the pull of Drew's attraction was beyond anything she had ever felt, and she knew she would risk anything to be with him, even if only for a short time. Jana turned onto Upper College Road and drove slowly down the tree-lined street until she came to a small ivy-covered stone building. She felt her heart beginning to race at the sight of Drew standing outside near the steps as she slowed the car. Drew got in next to her.

"How did the talk go?" she asked, placing a hand on Drew's hand. He leaned over and kissed her softly on the lips.

"I think it went well. It was pretty crowded, and there were quite a few questions afterward."

"I'm so excited this worked out for us. At least you can see a bit of Newport. We're going over the Newport Bridge now. I always love this view."

"Yes, it's beautiful, and spending this time with you is beautiful and special," Drew replied.

As they drove along Thames Street, Drew took in the sights along the wharf. They pulled into a small parking spot under the outer stairs of her friend's bed-and-breakfast. Walking up a flight of stairs to the landing, Jana put the key in the lock and opened the door. A cozy apartment greeted them. They pulled back a flowered comforter and lay down together on the cool sheets. At first, Jana and Drew held each other, breathing in each other's scent and reveling in the feel of themselves against each other. Then, wordlessly, they undressed and began to make love. When Drew entered her, she felt she was the most special woman in the world. She realized that he had been the first person who had taught her how to truly love someone unconditionally and to feel that love in return. Jana's emotions flooded over, spilling in gushes of love for this man. This man, Monsignor Drew, who had led her into the most intimate place of his heart and soul and shared himself with her. Wrapped in the arms of his caring, she could not ask for anything beyond this moment. The moment, however, ended too quickly, as it was nearing time for Drew to leave. He sat up in the bed with her.

"I brought a poem I wrote that you might like," he said, turning and handing her a piece of paper. "You can read it after I leave and let me know what you think."

Tearfully, Jana dressed, and they departed for Kingston. They embraced and kissed once more. Then Drew walked into the house where a few of the other priests were waiting to take him back to New York.

There were times, like these, when Jana was afraid to even ask when she would see him again. She knew it wouldn't be soon enough. Driving back to Newport, Jana stopped at a little park not far from her house to read Drew's poem:

in light, god comes—a gentle beam to
pierce imprisoning walls of power and
fear in peace, god comes—a truth sayer
to cleanse subtle makeup that masks us
from ourselves in love, god comes—a
contradiction to loosen the bonds we use
to hold each other

CHAPTER 10

Inner Tornadoes

M ichael was researching his next film project and had decided to go overseas this time. The bulk of the shooting would take place in Italy. This was his first film out of the country, and it was somewhat of a risky undertaking, but he could not resist the story line. It was to be set in a small village in Sardinia and was essentially a mystery. The entire project would take about three months. Initially, Michael felt that the strain of being away from Jana for that long would be difficult. Lately, however, the prospect of being apart had not bothered him as much. There was something different about Jana these days. Something indefinable. It wasn't just that she was preoccupied with the center; it was more as if she weren't even aware of his presence. He expected that she would be happy to have him at home and would make time to do things together. Instead, it was as if they were leading separate lives. *Perhaps it's just because we are used to being apart*, Michael thought. Yet Jana had not seemed interested in even going out on their friend's boat or in doing any of the things she had clamored for him to do in the summertime. She did not seem interested in his ideas for the new movie in Italy, and she'd always shown enthusiasm for his new projects. Even his suggestion that she come and spend time in Italy with him, a place she had wanted to visit, met with little expression of interest.

———

One afternoon in mid-August, Jana was putting on the final touches at the center. She'd hung pictures, the carpeting was down, file cabinets were in, the massage tables were in the rooms, and most of their supplies had arrived. Shelves were stocked with massage oils; candles; towels; wet heat pads; ice packs; and soothing CDs of whale sounds, the ocean, the woodlands, and chants. A few showers had been installed. The front room would be used as a dance studio, and a barre had been installed along with a wall-length mirror. Here, they would also hold meditation classes. A part-time certified massage therapist had been hired.

Jana walked through the rooms smiling with satisfaction. This was their dream come true. The ringing of the phone broke through her thoughts.

"Hi, honey. How is it going? Want to meet for dinner?" Michael asked.

"Sure. Where?" Jana asked.

"Let's go someplace special tonight. We haven't done that in a long time. There's that new place next to Christie's, the Sandpiper. It has a beautiful view of the harbor, and we can sit outside, as it's warm enough. Can you make it by six? I'll go ahead and make reservations."

"Sounds great. I'll meet you at six, then. Bye, honey."

They sat at a table looking out over Newport Harbor. There were a number of bobbing yachts and sailboats moored at this time of year. The Sandpiper was a new upscale restaurant that catered to the vacationing yachters. Dinghies brought the vacationers to restaurants along the harbor and dropped them at their boats afterward.

"It would be nice to have a small boat to go out in the harbor every now and then when we wanted," Michael said. "I remember going out on my dad's boat in La Jolla growing up. I've always loved being on the water."

"I think we're too busy for that. You're not here enough to take care of a boat, and I have the center now," Jana replied.

"I guess you're right. Maybe we should get a dog instead."

"A dog? If we don't have time to take care of a boat, how would we take care of a dog, Michael?"

"Oh, they pretty much take care of themselves. I guess I'm just feeling the need to be more grounded here somehow. I … I feel sometimes like we're slipping away from each other, leading separate lives. We don't share as much together anymore. It's hard to get close to you lately. And, well, to be honest, you seem to care more about the center and Leah than you do us."

"That's not true, Michael. I don't love anyone the way I love you. You mean the world to me. You know that. And you're the one planning another project in Italy now, for God's sake!"

"True, but most of the time, you seem a million miles away anyway. I think Leah and the center mean the world to you and I am an afterthought scheduled into your life at your convenience."

"Michael, you knew that starting this business would consume much of the summer, much of my time. I have to invest time and energy if I want this venture to be successful. Of course Leah and I spend a lot of time together. We're business partners. And yes, she is a close friend. I am not going to sit here and defend myself against your unnecessary insecurities."

"OK, fine. But I think the fact that you're getting so upset right now shows you know I am right."

"Michael, I don't want to discuss this anymore. Can't we just have a nice dinner?"

"Sure. Fine. We won't discuss it anymore. But I think you and I both know that things are not the same between us, not the way they used to be."

That night, Jana lay on her side of the bed wondering whether Michael suspected her relationship with Drew or perhaps her increasing affection for Leah.

Summer began to wane. The back deck was finished, and Michael and Jana entertained friends there a few evenings throughout August. Jana and Leah started to receive their first referrals after an exhaustive marketing campaign that involved networking with all their friends and acquaintances. They had business cards made and advertised in the local newspapers as well. They took off a few days here and there to spend at the beach, as late summer was the best time to go. The ocean had finally warmed up. The two spent a few afternoons along Thames Street near the harbor checking out all the tourist shops and going on a little celebratory shopping spree, as their new center was now underway. Leah and Jana popped in and out of little cafés enjoying the sea air and sunshine, munching on little treats and enjoying themselves immensely.

Finally, autumn stole on them gently and gradually with chillier mornings. It released energy evident in people's days. Folks seemed motivated in the fall. More got done in less time. New projects were created. Vacationers left town. Children went back to school. And Michael began to prepare and pack for his overseas trip. He and a small group of coworkers would leave in a week. During that last week, there was little communication between Jana and Michael, both busy in their own lives.

On a dismal late-September afternoon, Jana drove Michael to the airport. Michael inhaled a cigarette. The ride reminded Jana of one they had taken a few years earlier, on their first trip to Newport, when they had argued and a tense silence ensued for much of the trip. It felt that way now. It was as if they were in a state of limbo. She did not know what to say or what would happen next in their lives. At the Providence airport, they sat and waited quietly, lost in their own reveries about what was to come. Jana felt a bit guilty, as she realized part of her was actually looking forward to having the house to herself again. It was almost a relief. She sensed that Michael did not feel the same. He seemed sad at the prospect of their separation. When it was time to board the plane, Michael embraced Jana warmly.

"I'll call when I get in and settled," he said.

"OK, have a safe flight. I love you." For she truly did love Michael despite their growing separation.

Jana could not know that Michael sat on the plane with tears welling up as he felt the sudden but familiar realization that it would be a while before he would see her again. He would try to put the thought out of his mind and concentrate on the short flight to Boston, where he would connect with his colleagues.

Jana felt a lump in her throat as she drove home. *It's as if I'm saying goodbye to Michael as we once were and will never be again*, she thought. At home, Jana walked slowly through the house looking carefully at each room, trying to measure how much of Michael was present, how much evidence there was of his existence in her life. Perhaps there was not enough, but she decided she couldn't think about this right now. She needed to talk to her best friend.

"Hey, Cam. It's me. I haven't heard from you in ages."

"Hey, Jana. How are you? How's the center project going?"

"Oh, it's great. We actually opened before schedule, toward the end of August. We've been slowly getting customers through word of mouth. I can't believe it is finally happening. Leah and I are going to celebrate the opening after our first one hundred customers—maybe take a trip somewhere.

"You go girl! And how is Michael?"

"Actually, I just got back from driving him to the airport. He left for Italy this morning. That's part of the reason I'm calling. I'm just really feeling at loose ends about us. I've actually been developing some strong feelings toward Leah. I'm finding that I think about Michael less. I'm so involved in the center now. And Leah and I usually wind up spending our free time together. I think Michael suspects our feelings go beyond just friends and business partners. Being in the airport together this morning was painful."

"I knew it! I knew it was just a matter of time before this would happen. The way you talked about her and described her."

"Well, I do think about her and enjoy spending time with her. I can't tell anyone about my feelings except maybe for Adrienne and you."

"I know. That's how I feel about you. I'm glad we've been friends for all these years."

"Me too. So ... I don't know what I'm going to do. With Michael gone, maybe I'll be able to sort out my feelings."

"Will you go visit him while he's in Italy?"

"I don't know. I think we really need the time apart, and he's not going to be gone that long. Two or maybe three months at most. It will go by quickly. What's going on with you?"

"Same old, same old with Frank. I think the roller coaster is getting smoother now, finally. It's like I'm running out of energy to correct him any longer. I think I'm beginning to accept him for who he is."

"Well, that's good, isn't it?"

"Yeah, I guess. But he just doesn't get it. And I don't think he ever will. Anyway, I'm still planning to fly up for a visit this fall, if we're still on."

"Absolutely! I'm looking forward to it. I have big plans for us. Frank is still working on weekends, right?"

"Yes. What's Leah doing?"

"I don't know, but she is always busy with something. It will be fine. You can meet her if you want."

"Ye-ah, of course I want to meet her. I want to check her out big-time, see if she's really your type!"

"Okay, let's see how much time we have first."

They hung up, and Jana decided to go for a walk. She drove her car near the Cliff Walk and parked. She liked to walk because it cleared her head. Plus, it was a gorgeous day. The breeze along the path was perfect. She reflected on how far her life had come and how different it was since she had lived in Manhattan. Many things she had wished for had come true. But life was never simple. There was always something complicating it. In addition, Jana still felt like something was missing. That feeling of longing was still there in the back of her mind. She wanted to travel. There was a force that drew her, a yearning that she couldn't explain. A desire that neither Michael nor even Drew could satisfy. For now, it would have to go on the back burner. She had made a commitment to the center and wanted to make it work. It really was a dream come true. The seagulls squawked and screeched overhead. Ocean spray caught the sun's light. People smiled and looked out at the ocean as they trod along the walk. *What a beautiful place!* Jana thought. She would have to get her bike tuned up this fall and start riding again. She was going to start a ballet class for children in which a few parents had shown interest. She felt blessed not to be captive to a nine-to-five routine. *I just need to take it one day at a time, and things will fall into place*, she told herself. But she knew, deep inside, there were inner tornadoes brewing.

CHAPTER 11

—∿∿⟋⟋⟋⟋⟋∿∿—

Robert Marsh

A few days later, Jana arrived home from the center and, checking her messages, saw that her father had called. Robert Marsh tried to keep in touch with his daughter as much as possible, and the few times she had been down to New York, she had managed to squeeze in a visit. He had been promising to make a visit to Newport. She decided to call him now.

"Dad?"

"Jana! Hi, honey. How are you?"

"Good, Dad. I got your message. Are you really coming up?"

"Yes! I have a few days free from work, and I thought I'd come and see my firstborn child!"

"Ha! I'm your *only* child."

"Yes, I know. I guess I just have to make the best of it!"

"Dad!"

Mr. Marsh laughed. "Honey, you know I'm just

kidding. Honestly, how would it be if I flew up this weekend? Are you busy?"

"Not at all. Michael is in Italy; I'm here alone. I'd love a visit."

"Okay. It will probably be Friday evening. I'll take a cab from the airport."

"No, Dad. I can pick you up. It's no bother, really."

"Are you sure?"

"Yes, it will give us a bit more time together."

"All right. I'll call you with the details in a day or two."

"Great, Dad."

"Bye, honey."

Jana hung up the phone feeling elated. She hadn't seen her father since her last trip to New York several months earlier when she'd visited Drew. He was working now, in addition to his writing, as a reporter for a prestigious newspaper in New York City. She could use a friend right now with all the strain between Michael and her.

Robert Marsh was a reserved man. He was crazy about his daughter but expressive with few other people. He quietly sized up people and situations. A born writer, he expressed his opinions and ideas through the written word. He was relatively well off, having published a few novels. Recently he had been offered a part-time position as a reporter. He'd jumped at the chance because although being a published writer had its merits, he was often lonely and missed the company of fellow writers. Writers had a wonderful repartee among themselves, as he'd discovered in his early years as a reporter. Beyond that, ever since he'd lost Jana's mother, there had been a void in his life that no one had been able to fill. Mr. Marsh was tall, with short gray hair, and he kept himself in good shape through daily exercise. Although in his sixties, he was still a handsome man. Jana had inherited her good looks from her father, as well as his sense of humor. While a creative man, Mr. Marsh had somewhat unbending opinions and ideas about things. He was actually quite conservative. Jana did not feel she could even broach her feelings about either Drew or Leah with her father. However, she could share her struggles with Michael. It would be nice just to have him around for a few days.

Friday evening was a typical damp and dreary one as Jana made her way through the rain to the airport. She pulled into the arrival area and alongside the curb. Mr. Marsh was standing with his overnight bag and dressed in a black raincoat.

"Hi, sweetie!" he exclaimed as he got into the car, and he leaned over and gave her a kiss.

"Hi Dad. Have you been waiting long?"

"Nope, just got here, perfect timing."

They chatted on the way to Newport about Jana's center and how business was going, her father's work, and people in NYC whom she missed. As they came into town and made their way along Ocean Drive, Mr. Marsh commented that he had forgotten how damp and foggy Newport could be. Once inside, he put his bag in the guest room and made himself comfortable. Jana made some fresh coffee and started a fire in the fireplace.

"It's still early enough if you want to go out for dinner, Dad, or should I just put something together?"

"Let's just go out. I don't want you to go to a lot of trouble."

"Are you sure? I have some excellent soup, and Rosa went shopping yesterday, so there's plenty of food. I can heat up something. It won't take long."

"Whatever you want to do is fine with me."

"Okay. I was thinking maybe we could take a ride up to Barrington tomorrow and I could show you around the center. I would love for you to see the place."

"Sure. That would be wonderful. What's the name of it again?"

"The Barrington Balance Center. Dad, do you want to lie down and rest for a bit while I get dinner ready?"

"I think I will take a little rest."

Mr. Marsh went into the guest room and took off his shoes. He lay down on the bed, looking up at the ceiling for a while, and then closed his eyes. He thought of how proud he was of his daughter. After all, she had a beautiful home and a successful business. She was a talented dancer and teacher. She was a good writer. He wondered, though, about her relationship with Michael and how she dealt with all the separations. He could not have dealt with the separations as she did and believed that if his daughter would only marry and perhaps start a family, Michael would not be gone so often. But it was her life, and he did not want to interfere. Before long, he drifted off to sleep.

Jana put out plates on the dining room table, where there were fresh flowers, as always, Rosa's thoughtfulness in action. She had also telephoned Leah to say that her father was coming for the weekend. They decided she would meet them at the center and both would show her father around. Jana wanted to introduce him to her business partner and have a brief visit.

"Everything looks great, honey," Mr. Marsh stated as they sat down to dinner. "The house is just wonderful. I know I would never tire of this view, looking out at that mighty ocean."

"Thanks, Dad."

The two of them ate and chatted about Mr. Marsh's new position at the paper in NYC.

"I think this is going to be a good move for me. I'll have more energy and do more. Being without your mother has been difficult. Now I will have a camaraderie of sorts at the office, and it's just enough. The deadline is still the worst. There's still that pressure to get the piece in on time."

"I remember, Dad. When you worked at the *Daily Chronicle* when I was a teenager, I would call you accidentally at deadline. You'd hang up on me!" Jana laughed.

Mr. Marsh laughed as well. "I remember, sweetie, but you always called at the damnedest times."

Jana described Michael's new venture in Cagliari, Sardinia, and what it was like with him being away.

"I'm okay. He calls almost daily, and I'm busy with the center and my other work. But ... to be honest, Dad, Michael and I don't have the same relationship we did when we first met. I know that things change over time, but I think we are drifting apart. I feel he still loves me, but I didn't realize how hard it would be to make it work when he is home so rarely."

"I'm not surprised to hear these feelings, Jana. For my part, I could not imagine a life with your mother with long periods of separation. I think it would be challenging for anyone. Can you go and spend some time with him in

Italy while he's working on this film? Or have you talked about his doing films closer to home?"

"It's complicated, Dad. We're both trying to follow our dreams. I guess I could make time to fly out and be with him, travel a bit around Italy. We'll see."

They went into the living room, and as was his habit, Jana's father perused the bookcase and selected a book. He sat down comfortably in an easy chair and began to read. Jana finished in the kitchen and joined her father in the living room, where she sat gazing into the fireplace and thinking about the days when she was a child. How comforting it was recollecting the feeling of being taken care of and basking in the knowledge she was safe and protected—the innocent days when life was simply living from one moment to the next and right now was all there was. She felt that now, just a flicker of a memory of those early days, evoked by the presence of her father.

Mr. Marsh cleared his throat. "It's been a long day, dear. I think I'll turn in." He kissed his daughter good night and went into the guest room.

"OK, Dad. I'll see you in the morning. Don't forget: you're making breakfast!" Jana's father had always enjoyed cooking breakfast for her on weekends.

She sat for a while thinking about the oncoming winter months and how the weather would become windier and chillier as time went on. Thanksgiving would be here before she knew it, and Michael had already told her he wasn't sure whether he would be home. She might have to make other plans, as she didn't relish the idea of being alone. But for now, it was great seeing her father and spending the weekend with him.

Mr. Marsh arose early the next morning to a brilliant sun sparkling off the ocean. He dressed quickly and slipped out of the house and onto the front path. Though it was windy, he enjoyed the freshness of the salty sea air filling his lungs. He took a brisk walk along Ocean Drive for about a mile and back. He enjoyed watching the sea spray off the jetties as he walked. Joggers were already out, gloved and hooded against the wind. Back inside, he showered and dressed and then made his way to the kitchen. Jana loved pancakes and sausages, and her father loved cooking, so he prepared a nice spread with some fresh fruit as an appetizer. The two sat at the table chatting and enjoying a breakfast that reminded them of old times. Later that morning, they drove up to Barrington to see Jana's center. Leah was already waiting for them. Jana and Leah showed Mr. Marsh around the center, explaining the various rooms. He was impressed with what his daughter and Leah had created—the massage rooms, dance studio, and meditation room. He was especially impressed that their business venture was paying off. As was his style, he made a comment about Jana leaving the social work profession for something more lucrative.

"It was nice meeting you, Leah," Mr. Marsh said, "and I am so glad you and Jana are working well together and the business seems to be successful."

"It was nice to meet you too, and I hope to see you again soon," Leah replied.

In the evening, Jana and her father went to dinner at the Pier on the waterfront in Newport. Afterward, Mr. Marsh lit a fire back at the house, and they sat in the living room, he with a book propped on his lap while Jana went through some mail and paperwork. The next day, they sat quietly at the dining room table, eating lunch and listening to the sound of the robins chirping through the open window.

"Honey, why don't you come down to New York for Thanksgiving?" Mr. Marsh asked.

"I'm not sure if Michael will be home or not. I guess we could come together if he is, and if not, that would be nice. I could make plans to see Adrienne and John again as well."

"Good. Then it's settled. It will be a good time."

CHAPTER 12

—⁓⦿⦿⦿⦿⦿⁓—

Suspicions

In Sardinia, Italy, Michael was settling into his new life. How different from Newport and yet in some ways similar. They were both islands, and both had active ferries at one time or another. Michael and his crew had spent a few weeks scouting and decided on Cagliari. It seemed that the towns closer to sea level were more interesting than the ones in the hills. It was also too difficult to haul the movie equipment to the higher elevations. And then there were the markets. A friend had told Michael that the markets of Cagliari were spectacular. Their fruits and vegetables, their meats—all were abundant and delicious. As there would not be much to do in the town, they could at least eat well. While Cagliari was a bit remote, it afforded them a good deal of privacy while shooting. Michael had been studying Italian before his departure. He wanted to be able to communicate with the locals.

Initially, things went fairly well. Michael and

Jana exchanged regular phone calls about how their new ventures were progressing. Both were filled with excitement about their new projects.

One evening, Michael called to check in as usual.

"Hi, honey. It's me. How are you?"

"Hi, Michael. I'm doing great! How are things going there? Are you fluent in Italian yet?" she teased.

"Ha! Far from it. Still a big learning curve! Things are okay. I'm a bit lonely. The shooting is going well; we're on schedule. Everybody is doing well. I … I've just been thinking about you."

Jana reflexively responded, "I've been thinking about you too." She wasn't sure whether that was true but didn't want to hurt Michael's feelings.

There was a pause, and then Michael said, "Jana, there's something I need to ask you. I'm not sure how to ask this question. But I—"

Suddenly the line was filled with static, and the phone went dead. It was one in the morning in Italy, and unfortunately the location where Michael was filming did not have the best reception. Occasionally they got disconnected. Jana put the phone down. She paced around the room in anticipation of what Michael was about to ask. Maybe he wouldn't call back—maybe he couldn't call back. Jana got a drink of water. The phone suddenly rang.

"Sorry. It's those damn lines again. Lately the reception has been terrible. Are you there?"

"Yes, I'm here."

"Okay, well, I guess I will just come out and ask you."

"Ask me what?"

"Is there something going on between you and Leah?"

"What do you mean 'is there something going on'?"

"I think you know what I mean."

"Michael, what are you talking about?"

"I'm asking you if Leah and you are involved."

"Involved?"

"Yeah, are you having an affair with her?"

"Are you crazy? Why would you ask something like that?"

"There are many reasons I can think of, Jana. The way you get so excited when you know you are going to see her. The way you act around her. The fact that you talk about her all the time. The fact that you're not home late at night sometimes when I call you. I could go on."

"Please don't. I think you are overreacting from being away from me. Nothing remotely like that is going on between Leah and me. I told you I enjoy spending time with her, and she *is* a great friend with whom I have a lot in common. We are also business partners. As far as not being home late at night, I've already told you that sometimes I turn the phone off, and occasionally when Leah and I have been out late, I just wind up staying there. I don't like to come home to an empty house; you know that."

"It's more than that. I'm convinced of it."

"Well, if you're convinced of it, there's nothing I can say except you're being irrational."

"Fine, but I've decided I'm not coming home until Christmas. I think you're hiding this from me, and I just don't want to be around you right now. I feel you could easily betray me without giving it a second thought."

"You sound so angry, Michael. Have you been drinking?"

"Maybe. That's not the point. I have to go now."

Jana put the phone down. Slowly she began to feel her world unraveling. Wasn't it only a few years ago that she had been happy in a wonderful relationship with a man she adored? Wasn't it only a short while ago that she had moved to Newport and bought her dream house in a gorgeous seaside town, leaving behind the ugly aspects of New York? Her dreams had been realized. Now Jana felt miserable. Life did not fit so easily anymore. She thought back to her childhood, to the crushes she'd had on older female classmates and teachers. They were sometimes intense, sometimes fleeting. Even as an adult, she had selected as friends the beautiful women. In between boyfriends, there had been "interests" in other women. Her feelings about Leah seemed to be leaking out more and more, and she could no longer hide them. For most of her life, she'd cared too much about what other people thought. Now was her opportunity to live her life as she wanted. She poured herself a glass of red wine and sat on the couch wondering what to tell Michael when the next phone call came.

Jana found herself longing to see Drew again. She called his office in New York City.

"Full Circle. How can I help you?"

"Yes, hi, is Father Drew around?"

"Hold on, please. I'll check."

Jana's heart started to race with anticipation.

"Hello?"

"Drew? It's Jana. I'm so glad I got you!"

"I'm so glad you got me too," Drew laughed. "I was just leaving to give a talk. How are you?"

"I'm good. Michael is in Italy, and I really need to see you. Can you make some time?"

"I'll be flying out to Denver to give a talk next week, but I could find some time this weekend if you could come down.

"Yes. When? Where can we meet?"

"I can meet you at Penn Station if you're taking the train. How does tomorrow afternoon sound?"

"What's tomorrow? Oh, Friday. Okay. I'll take a morning train in. Should I just call when I get there? I will probably be around noonish."

"Yes. That's good. See you then. I love you."

"I can't wait to see you. Bye."

Drew always told Jana he loved her before hanging up—something Jana could never quite get used to. She wanted to say it back but couldn't.

On the train ride to NYC, Jana let her mind wander. *Would Drew ever leave the priesthood for me? If he did, could we have a baby? Would I really leave Michael?* She already knew the answers—that it was all an impossibility—but still the strong feelings for Drew were there, stronger than ever before. The train sped along, Jana watching pine trees whisk by and considering how to broach her feelings with Drew.

As Jana went up the steps into the station, she immediately saw Drew talking with someone while leaning on the side of the marble column. Her heart began to race as always; there was no better feeling than looking at him.

Drew approached her and leaned over to kiss her on the lips. She noticed the perspiration beading near his temples. His dark hair and temples were damp. She felt his strong arms embrace her. She pressed herself against him and breathed in his scent, his sensuality.

"How are you? How was the trip?" Drew asked.

"Good." She couldn't say much more when first meeting Drew, as she found herself always a bit nervous.

"The car is just outside."

"The car? Whose car? Drew, you don't even have a driver's licensc."

"I know. It's all right. I tell them I'm a priest." Drew smiled.

The two drove off down Lexington Avenue, with Drew smoking and seeming to be in good spirits. "Want to get a bite to eat?" he asked.

"Sure. Where can we go?" Jana always worried about where they could have a meal without being too out in the open.

"I have a place," Drew said confidently.

They drove for a few minutes and then pulled into a questionable parking spot.

"Are you sure it's okay to park here, Drew?" Jana asked.

"It's fine," Drew answered.

Drew held the door open for Jana as they walked inside. A man in an apron rushed over, welcoming Drew and shaking his hand. They exchanged some pleasantries and were led over to a table in a corner. Drew ordered a beer and a corned beef sandwich. Jana ordered a hamburger. In that moment, she realized that she had never paid attention to what Drew ordered—nor did she pay attention to much of what was going on his life, or even ask. She was too mesmerized by his presence. But Drew always asked about her and listened patiently to her struggles with Michael, her happiness about the center and life in Newport. But she did notice today that Drew seemed to be coughing a lot. After paying the check, Drew ushered her into the car and drove to a nearby motel.

They quickly undressed. Jana looked up at Drew with anticipation as he rested his body against hers. How had she ever managed to capture this man of God into loving her in this way? Gratitude flowed through her body as they began to make love. Afterward, Drew kissed her softly.

She turned to him. "Do you think we could ever be together?

Drew leaned over and lit a cigarette, lying on his side and facing her. "No, I don't think so. What we have now is all I can really give you. I love you, and you are a very special person to me, but I have responsibilities that I cannot abandon."

Drew stroked her hair as Jana turned away and the tears began to flow. She knew this would be the answer, yet it still hurt to hear.

"It's just never enough. Your time is so limited. We hardly ever get long stretches of time together," Jana said.

"Well, maybe I can get away for a weekend sometime soon."

As it turned out, Drew was giving a talk on Long Island a few weeks later. Michael was safely ensconced in Italy, so Jana took advantage of the opportunity to fly down and join Drew. They drove out together from Manhattan for a weekend getaway. The sponsors put him up in a nice hotel. After checking in, Drew had several calls to make, so Jana entertained herself with a book.

"I have to go and meet with the other speakers, but it shouldn't be too long," Drew announced.

It was always this way, Drew having to leave to go somewhere just when they'd gotten together.

Jana signed, "How long do you think you'll be?"

"I'll do my best to get back as soon as possible," Drew replied and kissed her goodbye.

Jana thought about the implications of their relationship. Would she tell Michael? Would she be found out? But just now, Jana did not want to think about those possibilities. She wanted to bask in the pleasure of their being together. But her conscience led her to calling Michael. Upon getting his voice mail, she left a brief message that she was checking in. After Drew's talk, he picked her up, and they drove to a restaurant close to the hotel.

"What was your talk about today?" Jana asked.

"It was really the same message I always try to give— that we all live to name life, of showing others the richness in themselves." Drew's organization, Full Circle, had a mission "to inspire the poor to become aware of their own resources and the potential beauty of the urban setting," as he put it.

They talked about Jana's interest in social work despite her having chosen another profession and about the important work Drew had done in Spanish Harlem. Back at the hotel, Drew was tired, partly from the day and partly from having had too much alcohol at dinner. He soon fell asleep, softly snoring. In the morning, he began searching for her, and they made love and held each other, both in a state of wonderful satisfaction.

Driving back to the city, Jana felt her mood plummeting.

Drew looked over at her. "I'm sorry we didn't have more time together. It was difficult to get even this amount of time. I'm always behind schedule and showing up late for appointments, but people seem to understand and are forgiving. I wish it could be longer too."

It was dark by the time they got back, and Drew parked the car. They kissed passionately until someone walked by and whistled. Jana got out of the car then and waved.

CHAPTER 13

—∾∿⌇⌇∿∾—

Yearnings

Jana began to think more seriously about her desire to visit India. After all, she thought, Drew had his life, and Michael had his career. She, too, wanted to realize a dream. Yes, the center was wonderful, but none of it was enough. There was always the nagging feeling that something was missing from her life. She had been thinking about it for a long time and was interested in visiting an ashram in Ranchi. Jana's mother had been interested in Eastern religions and had introduced Jana to Self-Realization Fellowship started by Paramahansa Yogananda. Jana had studied the lessons for years and felt a longing to see the actual ashram where Paramahansa had taught. She had several friends in New York City who were East Indian and had invited her many times to visit their families in India. They offered to travel with her to various places if she wished. She wanted to pack up the center and store everything for about three to six months.

Jana wanted to take Leah with her. She just didn't know how to broach the subject. However, if she really meant to go, she'd have to bring it up at some point.

Leah and Jana were having coffee at a café in Brick Market Place when Jana told her she was thinking about seeing the movie *The Insatiable Traveler.*

"I hear the cinematography is incredible. And they have shots of where Michael is filming in Italy."

"Where is it playing?" Leah asked.

"Just over in Middletown, at the Cineplex. Actually, I think this is the last week."

"Well, want to go, then?" Leah asked.

"Sure! Do you have any plans tonight?"

"No, tonight would be fine."

They jumped into Leah's car and drove up Broadway and onto West Main Road. It was a cloudy evening, warm for this time of year, in late September. Foghorns droned in the distance. The movie transported them to places they had talked of visiting. Jana felt a longing well up inside her to go to places unknown, uncharted territory. Places where ancient religions had sprung up, like Hinduism and Buddhism.

As they walked toward the parking lot, Jana said, "Leah, you know how I've become interested in the self-realization teachings of Paramahansa Yogananda?"

Leah nodded.

"Well, lately I have been increasingly drawn to the lessons and to the culture of India and really would like to make a trip there."

"Oh, well, when were you thinking of going?"

"I'd like to go soon, by November or so, which is the

best time of year to travel there. I'd like to stay for a few months traveling around the country. Michael will be away until Christmas, so this would be a good time."

"Things are just getting off the ground with the center, Jana. How could I possibly manage without you now?"

"I don't want you to manage without me. I want you to come with me. We could pack up the center or sublet it for a few months."

"Sublet it! Wow! I'd have to give some thought to this idea. It would be a huge undertaking. How would we manage financially?"

"We could borrow against the center. I know it would be tight financially, but we might bring back some new techniques and products that could enhance the business."

Leah agreed to think about it. She would have to take care of some business beforehand but couldn't help but be tempted by Jana's adventurous idea.

A few weeks later, Jana and Leah were folding and stacking towels from the dryer and putting them away in the closet.

"Wouldn't you be willing to wait a year? At least until the center is firmly established?" Leah asked. "It seems like such a risk to leave everything we've worked so hard for, just pack up and go when we don't even know how things will be when we return. I would need to find someone to look after Lolita and check on my place from time to time."

Despite Jana's urgent yearning to leave for India, she relented and agreed to wait until the next year. By then, Leah would feel more willing and confident about going.

In the meantime, Jana focused on the center. Their

massage clientele picked up, and Jana started a beginner's ballet class for adults, as well as one for children. In the afternoon, children scurried in accompanied by their parents to the dressing rooms, where they peeled off their outer clothes and became little dancing angels. Dressed in pink tights and black leotards with pink or black ballet slippers, they jumped around playfully while mothers attempted to put their hair up and off their faces. At the barre, personalities varied. There were those who stood solemnly, left hand at the barre, regarding their postures and positions. Others giggled with friends or made haphazard attempts to copy the positions Jana demonstrated. Although Jana always looked carefully for those who showed promise, she loved them all and embraced them as her dancing angels.

Leah assisted the massage therapist. She enjoyed the quiet, meditative quality of working silently with her hands to ease a person's aching muscles while they listened to the sounds of nature on various CDs. Leah and Jana taught a meditation class together in the evenings twice a week.

After locking up one night, Leah asked, "Do you have any plans tonight?" It was starting to get chilly in the evenings, and Leah wanted to get something warm to drink somewhere, as well as a change of atmosphere. Some days, they were working inside for ten hours if they were busy enough. Leah pulled her sweater tighter around her, the wind whipping her hair as she waited for Jana's answer.

"Camille is coming tomorrow, but sure, I have time to stop for a while. I just want to make sure everything is ready. I think the housekeeper came today, so it should be fine."

They went to a small nearby restaurant in Barrington. It reminded Jana of Eliza's, a little hole-in-the-wall she had frequented upon her arrival in Newport. There was a wonderful band that played jazz there. One day, she discovered to her dismay that they had moved Eliza's to Barrington. For months, she made the drive from Newport whenever she heard they were performing.

Jana began to shiver, and she and Leah were glad when the waitress came with hot apple ciders. The two sipped quietly for a few moments.

"What are you planning to do when your friend arrives?" Leah asked.

"Well, I know she wants to meet you. I thought I might take her to Christie's, and I know she likes the Mooring because we were there once before. You could meet us at the Mooring or Christie's for dinner if you're available."

"Yes, that would be great. I've heard so much about her and the pranks you two have been up to all of your lives! I'd love to meet her."

"Good. She's already been here, and we've done the Newport tour, so we'll probably just hang out and visit. I'll be at the center as much as I can in between spending time with Camille."

"Oh, don't worry about that. You've canceled your clients, haven't you?"

"Yes, but I hate to leave you with all the responsibility."

"I'll be fine. It's only for a few days."

They said good night and went to their cars. When Jana got home, she saw that Rosa had cleaned and straightened the house, putting fresh flowers in the vases. She ate something hurriedly and then lay down on the couch to read and think. Waking up hours later, she felt startled and lonely. She wasn't used to sleeping alone anymore without Michael. Morning came soon enough, though, with streaks of gray and blue colliding with the ocean in front of her view. Newport, like many seaside towns and islands, was more often damp and foggy than it was sunny. A stiff wind foretelling the beginnings of winter rattled against the panes. *Camille will be here in just a few hours*, Jana thought.

Jana huddled inside the Kingston train station house and watched through the window for Camille's arrival. Shafts of sunlight broke across the waiting room and the bench where she was seated. She heard the far-off toot of the train whistle and walked to the platform. Soon the women were embracing.

"Bana bear!" Jana exclaimed.

"Hola, chica!" Camille replied.

The two walked arm in arm toward the car.

"I am so glad you're here!" Jana said.

"Me too. That ride is a killer!" Camille exclaimed.

"Why, I thought you like the scenery and the relaxation of it, not to mention entertaining the passengers with your stories."

"Yeah, but four hours is more than enough," Camille said.

"Do you want to get something to eat?" Jana asked.

"No, let's just go back to the house. Maybe I'll have a cup of coffee or a snack."

"OK. I thought we might go out later to a really cool place around here, near the marina."

"Sounds good. Let's relax for a while. There's no rush. I'm really not that hungry. So … tell me about you and Leah," Camille said.

"Right now? I was going to tell you about what's been going on at the center and my classes."

"All right, but then let's get to the good stuff."

Camille had a way of making it perfectly clear that anything to do with relationships was her first choice of conversation, especially controversial relationships—her favorite.

"Well, the center is going very well. We've picked up a good, steady clientele, and Leah is getting some new regulars for massage."

"That's great. Has she given *you* one?"

"No. Maybe. We're not talking about that right now. I've started teaching ballet to the little ones, and, Camille, it is amazing. They are adorable. They're so cute in their leotards and slippers, and some of them try so hard. Others are just there to play. I love it! I could teach them every day."

"That's nice, honey."

"Don't be so sarcastic. I don't do that to you when you're telling me things that are important to you."

"No, true. I'm glad. It seems like things are going really well, and I'm happy for you. You deserve it."

Camille always ended her thoughts with whether or not people deserved things.

"Anyway," Jana said, "I'm not really missing Michael all that much, and he's probably figured that out."

"Really? How can you tell?"

"Well, OK, like when it's time to hang up, I never feel sad or desperate for him to stay on the line. I'm … content and I think he can sense that."

"So what are you going to do? Has he said anything?"

"Well, he has been hinting at it. And I'm not going to do anything. I don't want him to know a thing until I'm ready to tell him."

"You are sooo naive. Of course he knows. You said he already suspected that you and Leah were more than just friends before he left for Italy. You guys have been, like, dating in front of him."

"Well, I'm still not going to just tell him. Anyway, do you want to hear about my plans for the trip to India? It's in less than a year now."

"Yeah. How are you going to pull that off—leaving Michael, the center, the house?"

"I know, Cam. It's not going to be easy. I haven't said anything to Michael yet. We'll probably close up the center for the time we're gone, and I'm not sure about the house yet. Want to house-sit?" Jana laughed.

"Not me. I'm strictly a New Yorker—remember? But I wouldn't mind coming up in the summer if Michael's not around."

"Do you want some more coffee?" Jana asked.

"Yeah, that would be great. And I want to tell you about the latest with Frank."

The women talked for hours, sitting at the kitchen table drinking coffee and munching on snacks. It grew dark outside. They had taken off their shoes and changed into comfy clothes. Jana put her hair up. They looked at the clock: 9:00 p.m. They would have to order in now. This was a common occurrence. Nothing was more important when they were together than good conversation.

"Do you want to order Chinese or a pizza?"

"Pizza," Camille replied.

They ordered from the menu and moved into the living room. Jana set up the coffee table so they could eat in there more comfortably. They conversation finally shifted to Jana and Leah's relationship.

"So I don't really get it. How you two are different from, say, you and me? Well, I know the answer to that, but tell me more about what she's like."

"First of all, it's different in that I'm attracted to her. What she is like … hmm. She's gorgeous, intelligent, sexy, funny, and warm, with a soft way about her. All the things a woman looks for in a woman!" Jana laughed. "She loves the same things I do. We have a lot of common interests, and yet personality-wise we're very different. You'll see when you meet her. I have really strong feelings for her. I think about her a lot, hate being separated for more than a few days, respect her thoughts and ideas, and feel we make great partners."

"Wow! That's pretty intense. So … don't you think you should tell Michael the truth?"

"It's not that simple, Cam. I still love Michael. I'm hoping by the time he comes home from Italy in December, I'll be clearer about my feelings and have something concrete to tell him."

"Like 'Hi, honey. Welcome home from Italy. I'm leaving you for a woman'?"

"No. Of course not. At this point, I have so many

mixed feelings. I want to go to India. I would like Leah to go with me. But it's not easy leaving Michael and the house and the work at the center."

The women decided to call it a night and got ready for bed. Rosa had prepared the guest room for Camille. The next morning, they roused themselves from sleep around late morning. As usual, Camille enjoyed her morning coffee and blueberry muffin by the window seat overlooking the ocean.

"What do you feel like doing today?" Jana asked.

"Let's go shopping at those stores along the wharf. I wanted to look at the sweaters and a sweatshirt for Gary."

The women headed to Brick Market Place and then along the shops on Thames Street. Camille loved to go in and out of the shops talking to the salespeople. They looked at pottery; jewelry; and an assortment of other items, such as hats, bags, baskets, and glassware. Then they headed back into the throng of tourists milling around. Camille found a shop with some colorful sweaters and a shirt for Gary. Jana stopped in at the Chocolate Soldier for a Godiva sample that she had to have. They strolled along Thames Street, making their way to Lee's Wharf. Jana had a friend who owned an antique shop at the end of the dock. They went in to say hello.

"Girls, my goodness, what a surprise! Well, come in. I haven't seen you in months, Jana!"

"This is Camille—you remember. She came up a few months ago. Camille, this is Daphne."

"Oh, yes, yes. Aren't you the one that works with Jana at that center in Barrington?"

"No, Daphne, Camille lives in New York—remember?"

"Oh, yes, that's right. Brooklyn, isn't it?"

"Yes. You have a great store here," Camille said.

"Oh, do look around. Business has been so bleak, Jana. The winter months really kill us. This weekend, though, it's been picking up a bit. Jana, how is your center going?"

"It's going well. We're really pleased with it. We've got a great location right on the main street, so, yes, business has been good, thankfully."

Jana and Camille said their goodbyes and walked up to the Old Stone Mill, believed to have been built in the seventeenth century. Sitting on a park bench, Camille remarked, "What a beautiful town! I could totally live here."

"No you couldn't. New York is the only place you'll ever live."

"I know, but I wouldn't mind having a summer place here."

They returned to the house to shower and change for dinner. The Mooring was casual, so they changed into sweaters and pants and then headed out. Jana noticed when they arrived at the restaurant that Leah's Saab was already parked in the lot. Jana smoothed her hair, trying to settle her nerves as she realized that her best friend was about to meet the object of her admiration. She wanted the two to like each other, but they were so different she had doubts. As usual, Leah was waving and smiling cheerfully from the entrance as the two women approached. Jana and Leah embraced, and then Jana introduced Camille to Leah.

"Hi, Camille. I've heard so much about you from Jana. It's great to finally meet you."

"You too."

The waiter ushered them to their table, and they were seated. Camille immediately began to ask Leah all about herself, the center, and how she liked Newport and generally plied her with questions. Leah laughed and took it all in good stride. Camille observed Leah's easy way, her poise and gracefulness, and especially her resonant laugh. She could understand what Jana saw in her. Leah, for her part, was amused by Camille's quick wit, and the evening seemed to go smoothly.

"Jana tells me you two have been friends for over ten years. How did you meet?"

"We both got our master's degrees in counseling. I gave it up before Jana because I had a son. I also didn't feel I would have been any good at it. In the beginning, we were going to start a practice together—remember that, Jana?" Camille laughed.

"Yeah, 'Marsh and Mark Associates.' I remember. We had big dreams of becoming famous psychotherapists!"

"Jana tells me you have several artist friends and work part-time at a gallery in Brooklyn."

"Yeah, I'm really good at the sales-and-schmooze part, not so much at the art part! But Brooklyn has really become a mecca for artists, and it's nice being a part of that world."

They continued to chat over brewed decaf until Leah finally said she needed to get home. Jana was anxious to hear what Camille's impressions were, and so they said their good nights and went their separate ways.

"Well, what did you think of her?" Jana asked.

"I can see why you like her; she's definitely your type.

She's very attractive and calm, just what you need. And she is poised. You were right about that. I'm just not sure what she sees in you."

"Thanks," Jana replied.

"Well, she's way out of your league. I mean, she's beautiful. But I would say, hey, go for it!"

"And I am. I know I'm lucky, Cam, but she thinks I'm pretty cool too."

"Anyway, she's an interesting person. Coming from the Cape Verde islands—it's very exotic."

"Yeah, I think that's part of the attraction for me."

As they were pulling into Jana's driveway, Camille announced she wanted to get an ice cream cone. She had a weakness for ice cream that usually surfaced late in the evening. Jana turned the car around and headed toward the Newport Creamery, which would still be open. There, they sat contentedly in a booth eating their cones.

"It's a beautiful thing!" Camille exclaimed.

"What is?"

"Ice cream, of course."

They both laughed. It was so easy between them at times. Jana realized how much she appreciated Camille's company whenever she visited. She was saddened to think she'd be gone in a few more days. It was the kind of friendship in which one could simply look at the other and know exactly what she was thinking. Or they found themselves saying the same thing at the same moment.

Early the next day, they awoke with plans to go the Sachuest Wildlife Preserve in Middletown. Jana had taken Camille there before, and they'd seen deer and other wildlife that Camille wanted to see again. The nice thing about the preserve was there was an assortment of trails they could take. Today, they took the trail that ran along the seaside, where they saw various bird roosts in the rocks. Rabbit, an occasional skunk, and wildflowers made their appearance. Jana and Camille had bundled up, as the weather near the ocean was especially windy. The two watched the ocean spray hitting against the rocks as they made their way along the path. A few bird-watchers were up ahead looking through binoculars. It was a tranquil spot, and the two women walked in silence, content in their own thoughts. After a while, it grew cold, and they hurried back to the car.

In the evening, they decided to have dinner at the Black Pearl on the wharf, one of Jana's favorite spots. She liked to take visitors there because of the warm atmosphere and the view of the harbor.

For the last day of Camille's visit, Jana had gotten tickets to see Doris Duke's home on Bellevue Avenue, recently opened up to tourists. Altogether not unlike the other mansions along Bellevue Avenue, there were a few notable differences. The tour guide reported that Miss Duke had kept two camels on the back veranda. The camels could often be seen loping around the back lawn. Each room was magnificently decorated, and Camille was especially impressed with an original Renoir hanging in Miss Duke's bedroom. The view from the back lawn was spectacular, as they could see the Cliff Walk going along the fence in front of them. Finally, they managed to drag themselves away and out through the enormous iron-gate entrance. Driving along Bellevue Avenue, they passed

Bailey's Beach and rode along Ocean Drive until they were back at Jana's house.

Once inside, Camille packed her things in the guest room while Jana prepared a light dinner. Jana enjoyed entertaining and prepared a meal of caesar salad, some fresh fruit, and soft drinks. She brought their meal into the dining room, where they could look out at the ocean. Across the road, rose hips were still in bloom, and a few people walked along. The wind picked up, and hedges quivered. Whitecaps emerged on the horizon as the sun began to set. Jana dreaded late autumn, as she knew winter would be fast on its heels with frigid, relentless cold, wind, and fog. She shuddered at the thought of it.

"Do you have anything planned when you get back to New York?" Jana asked.

"Nothing special, the usual—work, and Gary's still around occasionally." Camille's son was grown now, and with a girlfriend, but stayed with his mother at times. "I've got to spend some time with my mother, actually. She's been complaining lately that I don't visit her enough. Do you ever miss your mother, Jana?"

"Yes, I think about her, but she died so long ago that it seems like an eternity now."

"I know I will miss my mom when she's gone because our family is small."

They chatted for a while about family, and Camille suggested Jana come to New York to visit her in Brooklyn. Jana said she would plan something soon. The two watched a video that evening of something Camille's son had done. Gary was an aspiring film writer, and this was his first effort, *Dark Matter.* Afterward, they discussed the film a while and decided to turn in early for the night.

The next day, Jana drove Camille to the train station in Kingston.

"Keep me posted on you and Leah and your plans for India!" Camille exclaimed.

"Of course," Jana replied. "Have a safe trip back, and don't cause any trouble on the Amtrak!"

Camille laughed, and the two hugged each other.

CHAPTER 14

Holidays

Jana went to New York to spend the Thanksgiving holiday with her father. Robert Marsh picked up his daughter at Penn Station, and they drove to his apartment on the Upper West Side. The old apartments in the area were often large and spacious, and Jana's father's was one of those. There were three large bedrooms, two of which he used for an office and a guest room. Jana put her things in the guest room and freshened up, and then the two of them went out for lunch at a local favorite of Mr. Marsh's.

Once they were seated, Jana said casually, "Dad, I've wanted to tell you that I am thinking of taking a trip to India. It's a place I've wanted to visit for a long time, and so many of my Indian friends here in New York have invited me into their homes in India."

"Well, that certainly would be an amazing opportunity for you. Tell me more about your idea."

"I'm thinking of bringing Leah with me. She's agreed

to go, and we would sublet the center for a few months. I have someone to look after it. It wouldn't be until next November since there are many plans we still need to make. You know how Mom always loved Paramahansa's teachings? How she would always have a weekly group meeting while you manned the telephone?"

Her father laughed. "Yes, I remember being chief doorkeeper and phone monitor! Is that why you want to go?"

"Not only because of the teachings but also to see this incredible country. When I listen to friends talk about their families' lives in India, I am fascinated to hear what it's like. It's exciting just thinking about going. And Michael will most likely be directing somewhere, so it's not as if I would be leaving him alone.

"Actually, Dad, I haven't told him yet. I just haven't found the right time to bring it up."

"Well, you know I don't interfere in your lives, but you do need to tell him at some point—and not at the last minute."

"I know, Dad, and I will."

"In any event, you have my blessing. I'm glad you're not going there alone. I'm sure you will have an incredible experience with a lot to talk about when you return."

"Thanks, Dad. I wish this whole year were over and I could be leaving now. I'm restless to get there, explore a new culture, a new spirituality. Maybe I'm just anxious and impatient. Michael is off having his great adventures, and I'm always stuck here. It's not that I don't love what I'm doing. It's just that I need a new challenge, a change."

"And you will have one, sweetie. You only have a year

before you leave and, I'm sure, lots of planning to do in that time."

"Yes, I know, Dad. You're right. I'm sure it will go by quickly as our plans begin to materialize."

The next day, Jana's cousin Adrienne and her husband, John, arrived to help prepare the Thanksgiving meal. While John and Mr. Marsh chatted in the kitchen, Jana and Adi set the dining room table. Jana confided in her cousin.

"Adi, I'm so grateful you and John are here. With Michael not coming home until Christmas, it's good to have some family around."

"Yes, and I don't get to see my favorite cousin very often! John and I feel the same way. Thanksgiving would be just the two of us this year, as his brother is visiting his wife's family."

With dinner ready, the four sat down at the dining room table, feasting their eyes on the delicious meal in front of them. A golden turkey with stuffing, sweet potatoes, green bean casserole, and cranberry sauce were laid out before them, along with apple-cider drinks. Robert Marsh's cat, Sebastian, sat close to his chair, hopefully waiting for some treats. But Jana's father had launched into memories of past Thanksgivings, when Jana's mother was alive and they'd all been together, and the cat's meows went unnoticed. After a lively dinner, everyone chipped in to clean up, and then John and Adi said their goodbyes. Jana and her father sat in the living room drinking coffee.

"Your mother knew how to prepare a Thanksgiving dinner like no one else. She always put the finest touches to a meal. Ah, well, time moves on … I'm glad we were able to be together this year, sweetie."

"Me too. Just being here is comforting instead of rattling around in my house alone."

Jana and her dad watched TV for a while and then said their good nights. Jana was eager to get an early start the next day.

———— ⁓⋆⊙⋆⊙⋆⊙⋆⊙⋆⊙⋆ ————

Jana arrived home, and her thoughts turned to Michael's impending arrival for the Christmas holiday. With Rosa's help, she began to decorate the house for Christmas. In between, she worked at the center and met Leah a few times for dinner. In mid-December, Michael flew home to Newport. He arrived in good spirits with several presents for her, as was his ritual. Despite Jana's worries about Michael's suspicions that she had more than just a friendship with Leah, he did not mention it, and Jana happily opened the gifts from him. They spent the next few days celebrating the holiday with friends. Leah stopped by for a quick visit, and they exchanged presents. Michael and Jana listened to their favorite Christmas music and went about getting adjusted to being around each other again. Michael seemed to be glad to be home and settling in comfortably. For the most part, they enjoyed each other's company. Michael regaled Jana with stories about his time in Italy. He described the breathtaking Amalfi Coast, Naples, and Sorrento and the ferry ride from Sardinia to the mainland when they took time off to sightsee. He had fallen in love with Capri, its natural beauty, the various colors of the sea, and the lemon and orange trees and promised to take her there one day. He imitated the different accents to her and the way he would pull extras from the streets for various scenes. Everyone had seemed good-humored and happy to be in his movie. Over the next several weeks, he spent time taking care of personal business and spending time with Jana. Most evenings were spent at home, except for the occasional dinner and movie out. They enjoyed sitting in the living room in the evenings, looking out at the view and sipping wine.

As the crush of Christmas parties and gift sharing subsided, after the decorations had been taken down and put away, there emerged an awkward silence in the house. While life went on as usual, there was an undeniable distance between Jana and Michael. Strangely, Michael had not mentioned Leah at all, and the conversations had been fairly mundane. One morning, a few weeks later, while Rosa was sweeping sand off the window seats in the spacious living room, Michael came in and sat next to Jana on the couch.

Michael had not seen his daughter in some time. She was now a freshman at UCLA and had called him over the months inviting him to visit.

"Why not have Andrea come out here for a visit? After all, I still haven't met her, and you could see your parents later on."

"Oh, so my parents aren't invited, then?"

"Of course they are. You're the one who says they complain they are too old to travel this far."

"It's true. They don't seem to want to come out east anymore. I suppose I could fly her out here, but I want to see how she is settling in at the university, especially since she has no other family here. I'd like to meet some of her friends, get a feel for the campus. Perhaps I could bring her back here with me for a visit."

"Oh, that sounds like a perfect idea, Michael! But how long do you think you would stay out there?"

"Just a few days."

"When do you want to go? It seems like you've only gotten back from Italy," Jana said.

"Honey, I've been home for three weeks. I'll have to go back to Italy soon to finish shooting. Now is the time to go if I want to see her and have time for her to visit with us."

Jana conceded that this was probably the best time for Michael to visit Andrea, so they agreed.

CHAPTER 15

—wwwⲟⲉⲧⲟⲉⲧⲟⲟⲱⲱ—

Andrea

The plane slowly circled LAX as Michael mentally prepared to see his daughter again. It had been two years. She was now a freshman in college on a student visa. Andrea stood at the gate anxiously looking over people's heads to get a glance of her father. He came toward her, and she noticed he had begun to gray around the temples. They embraced, and Michael held her out so he could take a good look at her. He saw Claudia's eyes in his daughter. They drove directly to Andrea's apartment in downtown Los Angeles. Andrea prepared a nice lunch for her father. She handed him a glass of chilled mineral water, as it was a humid day. Michael actually was grateful for the warmth after leaving a chilly thirty-four degrees. Grilled cheese with a pickle and chips was his favorite, and she offered fresh cut-up peaches for dessert. Michael was very pleased that Andrea had a roommate and they resided in a safe part of town. After Andrea gave Michael a tour of her apartment, they drove down to the campus.

"It's so big that at first I did not think I could manage, but then I found this Brazilian club with other college kids like me who are away from home. It has been a great support network for me. We can speak Portuguese and talk about home and the differences and similarities. I have met people from all over Brazil."

"That's great, Andrea. Have you given any thought to what you might want to do as a career, or is it too soon?"

"Actually, Dad, I was thinking perhaps about becoming a filmmaker. What would you think of that?"

Michael turned to look at her and smiled. "Well, I think that is very ambitious. It's a great deal of work, and you have to be willing to take risks, but if you really want to do it and are persistent, I think you could be successful. Following in the old man's footsteps, huh?"

Michael gave his daughter a squeeze as they walked back to the car and decided where to go to dinner. They ate in Los Angeles at a favorite restaurant of Andrea's, the Shore Inn, and went back to the apartment, as Michael was a bit jet-lagged. Over the next few days, father and daughter had discussions about careers, dating, and relationships. Andrea introduced her father to a few of her close friends, and they showed him their favorite haunts. Michael raised the topic of meeting Jana when they returned to the apartment one evening.

"How about flying back with me to Newport for a long weekend and meeting Jana? You've never seen Newport, and it's an amazing town. You haven't seen the house, and I could show you my neck of the woods."

"What does this mean—'neck of the woods'?"

"Oh, it's an expression that means where a person lives," Michael said and smiled.

"Oh," Andrea laughed. "I have actually been thinking about—no, *dreaming* for a long time about—going to Newport. This might work out, as I am almost on semester break."

"Great! Well, pack your bags, and let's do it!"

"Wait. What about Jana? She isn't even expecting me."

"It was actually her idea. She has been wanting to meet you for a while."

Michael called Jana to let her know Andrea had agreed and was excited to return with him for part of her winter break. He then called his parents to see how they were doing and to tell them that he was visiting with his daughter.

Jana was still working her regular schedule at the Barrington Balance Center, writing critiques for *Dance Magazine*, and teaching a few dance classes. She was also trying to save as much as possible for the trip to India in the fall. She called out to Rosa from the bedroom.

"Rosa?"

"Yes, Ms. Marsh?"

"Michael is returning with his daughter, Andrea, and I am going to be a nervous wreck! How will we get everything ready in just two days?"

"Don't worry, Ms. Marsh. It's no problem. I can get your house ready in one afternoon! For Andrea, I will order flowers, and we will have fresh fruit. What does she like?"

"I have no idea. I guess get whatever fruit is in season.

Order a pretty colorful bouquet—maybe pink and red roses."

"Okay, I will go do the guest room, and you will see this place will be ready in no time!"

"You are such a comfort, dear Rosa. I don't know what I would do without you. Would you also be able to cook something just for the first night? I would like to have a home-cooked meal for her. I'm really so nervous about putting something presentable together the night of her arrival.

"Just get whatever you want, and I will cook it for you, no problem, Ms. Marsh."

Relieved, Jana sat down on the bed to think about what it would be like to meet Michael's now college-age daughter. It would seem strange to have Michael's child staying at her home, she thought. She wondered what they would talk about and how it would go. Jana called Leah to tell her the news and that she would probably be tied up for the next week. Leah suggested that Jana bring everyone up to the center to see how it had grown since its beginning. They could go out to dinner afterward in Barrington. Jana agreed to the idea.

It was a crisp evening when the plane landed at Providence airport. Jana pulled up to the arrival terminal with anticipation. Michael ushered Andrea into the back seat before jumping into the front passenger seat alongside Jana. Andrea and Jana exchanged pleasantries, and Jana immediately recognized Michael in Andrea's face. She definitely had Michael's smile. Her English was also very good despite having been in the United States for only a few years. On the drive home, Jana asked Andrea about college life and how her and her father's visit had gone. As they neared Newport, fog was already settling in and made driving difficult. Slowly, they made their way along the drive to their house. As soon as Andrea emerged from the car, she commented on the strong scent of the salty sea air as the wind whipped up the surf. The lights from inside the house reflected on the dark exterior lawn. Inside, Rosa had lit a fire to warm the evening chill. While Michael showed Andrea around their home, Jana went into the kitchen to go over the dinner preparations with Rosa. The aroma of the roast Rosa had cooked filled the room. A short while later, there emerged a huge platter of sliced juicy meat, roasted potatoes, carrots, and broccoli. The three gathered around the dining room table to enjoy the feast. Michael lit some candles, which flickered occasionally as the wind came through the windows.

"Everything looks so good, and it's all delicious," Andrea said.

"I'm glad you like it. I wasn't quite sure what to make," Jana said.

"Oh, this is perfect. It's so nice to have a home-cooked meal and to finally visit you and my dad in Newport. You have a lovely home. I hope it's no problem for you that I'm here."

"Not at all. Michael and I have been looking forward to having you come and visit us for a while now."

After dinner, Rosa presented a dessert of strawberry shortcake. Michael, Jana, and Andrea sat around the table drinking Brazilian coffee that Jana had purchased for the occasion and enjoying dessert. When Rosa came in to clear the table, they all moved to the living room and sat around the fireplace. Andrea asked Jana about the Barrington Balance Center, and Jana described what she did there and explained how she'd planned for them all to drive up to Barrington to meet Leah for lunch one day that week. By the time Rosa left, everyone had changed into comfortable lounge clothes. Michael put on a CD of the *Moonlight* Sonata, and Andrea looked around feeling that wonderful, comforting sense of being safe and secure at her father's home. Michael suggested one of his favorite board games but had no takers, as Andrea was feeling jet-lagged and Jana was tired from a full day. They sat there awhile in silence just listening to the music, with their own thoughts, staring into the fire.

"I think I will go to bed now. It's been a long day," Andrea said and smiled, interrupting the silence.

"Of course," Jana said and escorted her to the guest room, making sure she had everything she might need.

"I think I'm going to call it a night also," Michael said.

Shortly afterward, Jana and Michael headed to bed. For some reason that Jana could not quite pinpoint, she suddenly felt a loneliness come over her. She and Michael had been estranged for so long that she did not even know how to connect with him any longer. The music had made her nostalgic, longing for the times when she and Michael had first met and the excitement of it all. In her sadness, she reached out for him in the dark, needing to make love, to cling to him as one does for comfort. They made love sensing that they had already lost each other. Afterward, Jana's tears flowed, as they often did when she felt the bittersweet memories of a lost closeness that could never be retrieved. The kind of closeness and ecstasy perhaps only experienced in youth, Jana thought.

Andrea woke to the sun streaming through her window and went to look at the ocean crashing against the jetty, spraying a light mist against it. It was warmer today, and the wind calmer, so Michael and Andrea decided to go around Ocean Drive so Andrea could see the mansions. She was impressed with the vastness of each home, as well as the various architectures.

"It's so interesting how some of the homes are so modern and others seem built ages ago," Andrea commented.

"Yes, there are those people who feel the need to modernize these beautiful homes, but the ones left as a sign of the times in which they were built are much more beautiful, in my opinion," said Michael.

They drove along Bellevue Avenue and down to Thames Street, where they stopped at Bowen's Wharf for lunch. Andrea looked around Brick Market Place, selecting a few gifts to bring back to friends and family. They strolled along the harbor looking at the boats and the afternoon sun reflecting on the bay. Michael took Andrea for a ride along the causeway out to Goat Island to see the yachts moored there.

"Dad, did you ever think of getting a boat?" Andrea asked.

"We did think about getting one, but I'm away so much it just seemed impractical. Your grandparents keep a boat in San Diego, and I used to go out with them as a child. Perhaps when you return to California, you can visit with them. I know they would love to meet you and take you out on their boat."

As they walked along the docks, Michael shared with Andrea little anecdotes about the time he had spent with her mother in Brazil. On another day, they took a walk along the famous Cliff Walk so Andrea could enjoy the incredible view of the ocean as the path jutted out along the sea. Over the next few days, the two spent time getting to know each other better over meals and chats at the house and on their drives. Jana also got to know Andrea as they sat up late in the evening, after Michael had gone to bed, drinking tea or coffee and chatting about life.

"I notice you have a swing in your backyard," Andrea said.

"Yes, when I was a child, we had a swing in our backyard, and it was very special to me. The yard was hilly, and I would swing out over the hill looking up at the sky and imagine what I wanted to be when I grew up," Jana laughed.

"I also have a swing at home in Brazil and used to do the same thing, swinging and looking out over the hills of our town."

Jana smiled. "You see, I knew we were kindred spirits!" By now, Jana was beginning to feel close to Andrea, like the young woman was the daughter she'd never had. "You're welcome to use it anytime."

On Sunday, Jana made arrangements for all of them to drive up to Barrington so Andrea could see the center. When they arrived, Jana unlocked the door, and they let themselves in. They walked through, with Jana pointing out the various rooms. There was the massage room with light blue walls, candles, and a CD player for soft music, as well as a room for yoga classes that had folded-up mats in the corner, light peach walls, and a CD player. There was also the dance studio, where Jana taught her little ones. Then she showed them the little kitchenette they had made in the back. Andrea exclaimed that it seemed wonderful and wished there were a place like it near her. Michael commented on how organized and finished everything looked compared to the last time he had been up, when they were installing new floors and fixing up the rooms. As they walked back through to the large main room, Leah suddenly entered with a big smile, the wind blowing her long dark hair in her face.

"Hi, everyone!" Leah exclaimed. "Have you had the tour yet?"

"I've just finished showing them around," Jana said.

"Great. Are you ready to go to lunch, then? I've made reservations at Deltourno's near the bridge, which has a nice view of the bay."

Introductions were made all around, and they drove off in Leah's car to the restaurant. The soup of the day was New England clam chowder, which they all ordered while considering the entrées. Each decided on a fish dish, choosing fillet of sole, cod, or flounder. Everything was fresh, and all the sides were filling. Leah asked Andrea about her life in Los Angeles and going to college there. She commented on the resemblance between Andrea and Michael. After a satisfying meal, Leah dropped them off at the center, and the three made the drive back to Newport. As they got closer to town, Andrea commented on the foghorns that seemed always to be droning in the distance. Jana explained that this was a part of their lives on the island, known as Aquidneck Island, especially when the fog came in quickly. The next day, it was time for Andrea to leave. Jana and Andrea embraced, and Andrea thanked Jana for her wonderful hospitality. Michael drove his daughter to the airport and told her he would contact his parents so she could arrange to have a visit to meet them.

CHAPTER 16

—⁓⁓⟨e⟩⟨⟩⟨⟩⟨⟩⟨⟩⟨e⟩⁓⁓—

Cousins

M ichael had now been home for months and had to get back to Cagliari to finish his film. The crew was ready to return and wanted to start shooting as soon as possible. Though Jana knew his departure was imminent, somehow she could not bring herself to tell him about her desire to go to India or her increasingly stronger feelings for Leah, and of course there would never be any mention of Drew. Over the next few weeks, Michael spent time taking care of personal business and spending time with Jana. They enjoyed each other's company, and for a while, things were calm between them and they were content.

Once Michael left for Italy, Jana got busy with her own agenda. She began to focus on finding someone to sublet the center for the following year. She didn't know how long the process would take to find someone whom they could trust and who would be interested in running such a place. Jana decided to have dinner with Leah later that week so they could begin discussing a time frame.

"Hi, Leah—it's me," Jana said. "I was hoping we could get together for dinner this week. Lots to talk about!"

"Sure! Would Thursday evening work for you? By the way, Andrea is a lovely and beautiful young woman. I enjoyed meeting her. She speaks English well. I was surprised."

"Thanks. Yes, I was too. Thursday would be fine. Do you want to come to Newport, or shall I come up to you?"

"Oh, I'll come down. There are so many more restaurants in Newport."

"OK. What are you in the mood for?"

"How about Salas?"

"Sounds good. I'll meet you there around 6:00 p.m."

After hanging up, Jana spotted a travel book Michael had given her about Sardinia and all the local sights. She relaxed on the couch with a cup of tea and read about some of the places he'd visited or where he'd worked. He had given her a bookmark with an inscription that read "My heart is in Italy but not whole without you here." Michael wanted Jana to come and see Italy. He'd said they could travel together after filming was complete. It would be spring and perfect weather for sightseeing. Although she found it romantic and alluring, she had put him off.

Jana resumed her morning meditation regimen and her studies of the lessons founded by Paramahansa Yogananda in his *Autobiography of a Yogi*. Her thoughts turned to India and the desire to see Paramahansa's ashram in Ranchi, India. She looked forward to sharing these plans with Leah.

The two women sat across from each other at a small table upstairs in the restaurant. Jana talked to Leah about her hopes and dreams for the trip to India, as well as the task of getting someone to rent the center while they were gone. They would start with word of mouth and then advertise in the papers, the *Newport Daily News* and the *Providence Journal.* Jana wanted to leave by the end of October, when the rainy season was over and the weather was not too hot. Leah still felt somewhat unsure about the prospect of going to India yet was curious and felt that if she didn't go with Jana, she might not get the opportunity again. In the end, Leah made up her mind that she would go with Jana to India, and they determined they would leave by early November at the latest.

As spring settled in with some consistency, Jana took the storm windows down, put in the screens, and brought the porch chairs up from the basement. She set a chair outside in the morning sun facing east and soaked in the warmth, scents, and sounds. She felt propelled to sweep the deck and work a bit in the garden, where daffodils and lilacs had sprouted. At least she could bring out her wind chimes, as the weather would not destroy them.

An unexpected but delightful surprise was a phone call from Jana's cousin Adrienne inviting Jana to come to New York City for a visit. Adrienne said they needed to catch up. Jana pondered the invitation. No one really knew about her plans to go to India with Leah, so perhaps this would be a good time to visit and tell the news in person. She called Rosa to see whether she would be available to check on the house while Jana was gone.

"No problem, Ms. Marsh. Just let me know when you

want to go, and I will check every day. I will take care of the mail and whatever else you need. Don't worry; go and have a good time."

Rosa was always so willing to help and easygoing. Jana could have offered the house to Leah, but Leah did not like to leave her parrot for long. Jana wondered what Leah would do with that parrot when they went to India. She phoned Leah and told her she was going to New York for a long weekend and asked Leah whether she would cover for her at the center. Leah assured her that it would not be a problem. She then phoned Adi, and they made the arrangements for her visit. She decided to take Amtrak and leave her car at the train station in Kingston. She wanted to have time to reflect on the twists and turns her life was taking. Michael called that evening.

"Hi, honey. It's me," Michael said.

"Oh, hi, Michael. How are things going?"

"Good. Getting back into the flow. Listen—I sent something in the mail for you, so be on the lookout."

"What is it? What did you send?" Jana had never been able to wait for a surprise of any kind and now pressed him.

"It will be there soon enough. Just call me when it arrives so I know you've gotten it."

"Okay. I'm heading to New York to visit Adi and John for a few days."

"Oh, well, that sounds like fun. Tell them I was asking for them. Have a great time. Love you."

"Love you too."

The next morning, Jana drove to the Kingston station to catch the train to New York City. She found a comfortable window seat and noticed the train was sparsely occupied. After putting away her carry-on bag, she leaned against the window and found herself thinking about Adrienne's work as a graphic artist. Adi had taken over one of the rooms in her and John's spacious apartment as her studio. There was a large table for drawing, and she had several containers filled with markers, pens, scissors, rulers, and charcoal sticks. She loved toys, and there was an assortment of little fun gadgets perched around the room. It was Jana's favorite room in the apartment, and the two often wound up spending the most time in there. Jana thought about how hard Adi worked, sometimes for weeks on end until a project was finished. Then she would take a vacation skiing in the Alps or traveling with John. Adi loved to ski. She was self-employed and loved it that way. John's work was similar, with his being an attorney; he often worked feverishly on a case and would have a break before the next one. Jana thought also about how she would tell Adi about her plans to go to India with Leah—how much she would tell, how much she would keep to herself. Soon, she drifted off and slept, waking up near the border of New York and Connecticut. The train pulled into Stamford station, and the doors opened. Suddenly, there was a cool breeze and a smell that brought Jana back to her childhood, the smell of the ice-skating rink and the nearby Stella D'oro bakery. The combination of the two reminded her of her ice-skating days when that scent, with the camaraderie of friends skating and laughing, was all that filled her mind. Childhood inocence. The absolute best, she thought. Jana took out the book she'd brought along, *Inner Peace* by Yogananda, and read for a bit. It was comforting and only made her more eager to travel to India.

Taking a taxi to Adi's apartment from Penn Station, she made excellent time. The doorman took her up to the eighth floor, which opened to a small foyer with a single apartment. Adi stood smiling broadly with the door open, her face flushed with excitement. The two embraced.

"You know, you still owe me a visit to Newport!" Jana exclaimed.

"I know, and I'm planning on it," Adi replied. "How was the train ride?"

"Oh, I slept most of the way. The time went by quickly."

"Are you hungry? Can I get you something to eat?" Adi asked.

"A sandwich and some iced tea would be great!"

The two sat at the kitchen table catching up on old times. Then Jana put her things in the guest room, took a refreshing shower, and changed into sweatpants. She found Adi in her studio working on an advertisement and logo for a sneaker company. Adi never seemed particular about the type of job she had as long as it was work. She gave her best no matter what.

"I'm almost at the end of this one, thank God," Adi said. "It seems like it has gone on forever. John complains that I don't spend enough time with him, doing things together, but I just can't when I have a deadline. Anyway, it worked out well that he had to go out of town on business so I can at least have time to do things with you guilt-free."

"In a way, even though I would love to see John, I'm kind of glad he's not here. I need to talk to you about a few things."

"Really? Nothing bad, I hope."

"Not really, just a bit complicated."

"Okaay ..."

"You know how I've mentioned my interest in the teachings of Paramahansa Yogananda and Self-Realization Fellowship?"

"Yes."

"Well, I am thinking of making a trip to India in the fall, to visit the ashram where he gave his talks and to sightsee. Leah has agreed to go with me. We are going to try to rent the center, and Leah will have to find someone to keep her parrot. Rosa may stay at the house sometimes unless Michael is there."

"Wow! That sounds fantastic. Will you travel all over India? Will you go to see the Taj Mahal?"

"I plan to, but here's the problem. I haven't told Michael yet."

"Why not?"

"Okay, here's the complicated part. Leah is coming with me, and I don't think Michael really likes her. In fact, he suspects that I am having a relationship with her, and if the two of us just leave, it will only serve to strengthen his suspicions."

"Well, are you having a relationship with her?"

"Sort of. I mean, I have grown very fond of her, and I guess I do love her, but I still love Michael and I don't want to hurt him, so I've been denying that there's anything between Leah and me. Actually, I may wind up staying there a while, and Leah may return earlier."

"Jeez, Jana, that's a lot of information in the last five minutes!"

"I know. And I'm sorry to just blurt all this out to you, but I don't really know anyone else I can talk to who would understand."

Prior to marrying John, Adi had had a brief affair with a woman in New York who was in the graphic design business. She understood how people could fall in love regardless of sex, religion, ethnicity, and other cultural and societal barriers.

"I think you have to tell him something—and probably the sooner the better."

"It's just so hard. The whole situation, not knowing how he will react to all of these changes."

That evening, Jana and Adi sat in Adi's studio talking about old times and recalling funny anecdotes about their grandmother and mothers. They stayed up late and wound up going to bed around one in the morning. The next day, Adi left for an early-morning run through the neighborhood. As the two ate breakfast on her return, they discussed plans for the day.

"Hey, Jana, how about the Museum of Natural History and the Hayden Planetarium?"

"Sounds great!"

Both places were in walking distance, and Jane never tired of the planetarium. She loved sitting back in the chairs and watching the dome change from one constellation to another. They walked around looking at the various exhibits and then stopped in the museum cafeteria for lunch. As they walked through one of the major lobbies, Jana noticed the buzz of people and registered how stimulating it was to be in New York again.

They discussed Jana's dilemma that evening, and Adi

advised her to talk to Michael and not put things off any longer. Adi talked about her latest projects as well and that, in general, things were going well. The next morning, Adi surprised Jana with tickets for a Tchaikovsky performance at the New York City Ballet. Jana was thrilled, as Adi knew she would be. After the performance, they went to an Indian restaurant for dinner. There was a palm reader there who read both women's palms. She predicted long lives for each of them and diverging paths for Jana in her future.

The weekend flew by with their exploring New York together. Jana noted restaurants that had changed hands, new stores that had replaced the old, nostalgic hangouts gone forever. Too soon, it was time for Jana to leave.

"Thanks for everything. It was all wonderful, especially seeing you, Adi." Jana smiled and embraced Adi in a hug.

"You're welcome for everything," Adrienne laughed, "and I know it's my turn to visit you, and it's on the list, kiddo!"

———~~∘∘e⊹⊚⊹e∘∘~~———

Instead of heading for Grand Central Station, Jana took a cab to Fifty-Ninth Street and First Avenue. She had secretly arranged to meet Drew at a specified time and date. He'd managed to fit her into his busy schedule, as he wanted to see her just as much. As she approached the meeting spot with quickened step, she saw a figure with a broad back in a dark blue shirt sitting on a bench just next to the tram that went to Roosevelt Island. It was him. Jana's heart soared.

Drew rose and embraced her. They kissed. It was always passionate and always bittersweet.

"How are you?" he asked.

"I'm better now that I'm getting to see you. I had a great time with my cousin. She's always so gracious. And how are you? You're still coughing. Have you seen a doctor?"

Drew smiled. "I have, and he tells me I'll be fine. Not to worry."

But Jana did worry. She noticed Drew had lost weight. "Are you sure?"

"Yes, I'm sure. It's just slight bronchitis, and he says I have to give up smoking."

Jana did not want to push the issue, so they talked about Drew's work and recent talks he'd given around the country. As he talked, Jana realized again that Drew was really a mystery to her. He did not talk much about his life, and Jana never asked about where he lived—or if there were others. It wasn't that she didn't want to know about Drew's life outside of their relationship. Yet she suspected there were others with whom he might be intimate. This feeling prevented her from asking too many questions and she preferred to have only a peek into the life of this man whom she adored. It was safer that way.

"I don't have much time; I need to be somewhere soon," Drew said.

"We never get enough time together."

"I know, and I'm sorry. I promise I will make it up to you the next time. We'll spend the whole afternoon together doing whatever you want."

"You promise?"

"I promise."

Jana shared with Drew her increasing desire to go to India and to visit the ashram in Ranchi. She told him of her plans to take Leah with her and her feelings for Leah as well. Drew was always so accepting of people and nonjudgmental, which was another trait about him she loved. Then he rose to leave. He held her in a long embrace—an embrace that lingered with her all the way home on the train ride back to Newport. She could still feel his smell, his rough hands, his touch, his warmth. She could still see his loving eyes, the wrinkles in his face and the ever-present look of tiredness.

CHAPTER 17

—◦◦◦◦◦◦◦◦◦◦—

A Loss

When Jana arrived at home, she found that Rosa had tidied up and put a vase of fresh flowers on the dining room table, as always. Jana thanked her for her help and picked up the phone to call Michael. She quickly filled him in on the events of her visit to Adrienne's. He, in turn, reported they were making good progress, and he anticipated being home within the next few months. He asked her again whether she would consider coming to Italy to see him. Jana told him she would consider it if they could both find the time, and they planned to talk about it again soon.

Leah called to say she had found someone to take over the lease for a year at the center. She was a Reiki-certified massage therapist whose boyfriend was going to be living in Providence for a year, and she wanted to join him. Her name was Carollyn Ogden, and she was from New Jersey. She also had a partner who could teach the yoga and dance classes. Leah could not believe the luck they'd had, and Jana, too, was thrilled with the news.

It was nearing the end of summer, and Jana began to feel the excitement coursing through her as she reflected on her upcoming trip. The morning sun was overhead as she sipped a hot drink and sat out on the front porch. She surveyed the horizon, where long freighters stood seemingly stationary, along with a few small sailboats. People were walking out onto the jetty. Joggers went along the drive in T-shirts and shorts. *What will the horizon look like from the coast of India?* she wondered. Jana thought about the things she would miss about Newport: her home; Michael, of course; the center; the familiar surroundings; foghorns forever sounding in the distance. But other aspects she would not miss. One could never get used to the wind. It was almost always there, blowing sand on beachgoers, blowing objects down. And the sand, seeping its way into all the nooks and crannies of the car and house. The damp, of course. A dampness that caused all her papers and magazines to slightly curl. Hand-washed clothes that took forever to dry. Yes, there were some things she would not miss. She decided she would need to tell Michael soon of her plans. For now, she busied herself teaching her dance classes and working at the center.

"Good morning, Missus Marsh," a chorus of five-, six-, and seven-year-olds said en masse as Jana ushered them to the barre.

"Good morning, my little dancers," Jana replied. "Let's start with our positions today. Who can show me first position? Good. And second? Now let's do third together. Very good, my little dance angels. Now fourth. And fifth." She put on ballet music and allowed the girls to make their own dance moves to the music as a warm-up. Leah arrived, and the women waved to each other as Leah walked back to the massage room to prepare for her first client.

And so the days went on. Jana and Leah worked hard and had a few meetings with the young woman who would take over while they were gone. With the anticipated trip growing ever closer, Jana began to think about what she would pack for her journey. She would need to plan for variations in weather, as her arrival time would be warm, but up in the mountains of Ranchi and in Nepal, the temperatures would be cooler. She would take some of her self-realization books, no doubt. She would also take a few sentimental gifts from Michael. Jana knew that it was essential to pack light, especially as they would be traveling to different cities. Her passport was good, but she would need some shots. She would also buy some sturdy luggage that would withstand such a trip.

While Jana was musing about her mental to-do list, she glanced over at the television. "And in other news, the well-known and charismatic leader of the Spanish Harlem community, known simply as Father Drew, passed away suddenly early this morning from complications stemming from pneumonia."

Drew's death left a gaping hole in Jana's heart from which she would never fully recover. For days, she was inconsolable in the loneliness of her grief. She had known Drew forever and couldn't imagine life without him. He was her confidant, the first real love of her life. She stood at the back of the enormous church where thousands had crowded in to pay their respects. The funeral was televised, and articles would later appear in the *New York Times* about his contributions to children and families. How proud she felt to have known Drew so intimately. Yet just at their intimacy had been a private matter, so was her sorrow. She approached the coffin and inadvertently reached out to touch his hand. She drew back suddenly as she felt the coldness. For days, she wept, thinking about the loss in her life and also in the lives of so many others. Jana felt that a light had gone out in her soul and she would never love again with the same passion she had for Drew.

CHAPTER 18

—~~∿∘⦿⊙⦿⊙⦿⊙∘~~—

Preparations

I t was September now—September 8, 1986 to be exact, when Michael called early in the morning.

"Hi, honey. Can you hear me?"

"Yes, hi, Michael. Where are you?"

"That's what I'm calling to tell you. I'm finally on my way home! We wrapped up filming last night, went out and celebrated, and I have a flight home tomorrow. I can't wait to see you, darling!"

Jana felt her throat go dry. She felt shaky inside. A wave of fear washed over her. "That's wonderful, honey," she managed to blurt out.

"I'm not sure exactly what time I will get in. I'll call you again when I have a better idea of my arrival time in Providence. I have so much to tell you!"

"I can't wait to hear all about the movie, Michael, and what it has been like there. And again, I'm so sorry I couldn't make it to Italy."

"I understand, honey. I know you have gone through a lot with Father Drew's death."

"See you soon, Michael."

"See you soon, honey."

And now the dread began. Jana was flooded with thoughts of how to broach the news with Michael. *Just do it!* she admonished herself. But already she could envision the dominoes of her life with Michael slowly cascading downward. For the moment, she tried to put these thoughts aside and look forward to his arrival. After all, she had not seen him in months. She missed him. She needed him. She needed to hold him and to be with him again. Jana called Rosa to give her the news, and Rosa came to the house later that day to help get things ready. In the evening, Jana tried to finish up a writing assignment and called Leah to let her know Michael was coming home. Then she went to bed. It was difficult to sleep. The outside world was still, the waves hitting the shore quietly, but Jana was filled with inner turmoil. The next evening, she drove to the airport to pick up Michael. This time, she parked the car and went inside to meet him. When she finally caught sight of him, Jana realized all over again why she had fallen in love with him. This handsome, charming, witty man was rushing toward her now, and she was going to leave him forever.

"Darling!" Michael swept her up in his arms and kissed her. "I've missed you so much!"

"Me too, honey," Jana replied. She looked at him lovingly, and tears welled up in her eyes.

"What's all this?" he asked with concern.

"I'm just happy to see you. We haven't seen each other in months. I'm glad you're home."

On the drive back to the house, Michael talked animatedly about the success of his picture and the relief of having finally finished the project. He told Jana about Cagliari, Sardinia, and the times they had gone into Naples and explored the nearby ruins of Pompeii. Jana listened with interest, interrupting with questions from time to time.

"How marvelous to have seen Pompeii—and just being in Italy. What an adventure!"

"Yes, I wish you could have come, but in any event, we're home together now."

They pulled into the driveway, and Michael quickly carried his bags into the house and flopped down on the couch.

"Come and sit next to me," Michael said, patting the cushion beside him. "I've brought you some small gifts from Italy."

Jana moved toward the couch and sat down next to him. A stir of emotions began to make her stomach feel slightly queasy. A wave of guilt spread over her. *How can I leave this man who loves me so?*

Michael had begun to pull out beautifully wrapped gifts from a bag. There was a gold bracelet, a pair of gold earrings, and a lovely ring.

"Oh, Michael, they're beautiful. I love them all. But I don't deserve them. I … I don't know what to say."

"Of course you deserve them. Who else would I give them to?" Michael laughed and hugged her.

Jana tried them on at Michael's urging while he

carried his luggage into the bedroom and began to unpack a few things.

He called out, "Honey, I'm exhausted. Let's go to bed. I just want to hold you."

Jana and Michael held each other close that night, both for their own reasons. For Jana, it was to feel his closeness once more before she would finally break the news of her imminent departure.

A few evenings later, Jana suggested they go out to dinner. She had been working up her courage and felt that in order to avoid an unpleasant scene, she would tell Michael about her plans in a restaurant. She chose one of Michael's favorites, one he had not been to in a while, in hopes that it would put him in a happy mood.

They sat at a table for two in the corner of the spacious dining room overlooking Newport Harbor as the sun was just beginning to set.

"Michael," Jana started in an earnest tone, "I need to talk to you about some things."

"Oh? You sound serious. Should I be worried?" Michael said half teasingly.

"Michael, you know how I've talked about the teachings of Self-Realization Fellowship to you a few times over the years?" Jana felt herself trembling.

"Yes," Michael replied a bit abstractedly.

Just then, the waiter came to take their order. Jana had no appetite but ordered anyway. She could always take it home later. Michael, on the other hand, seemed to have a voracious appetite this evening and ordered an appetizer along with his entrée, confiding that he was considering dessert as well.

After their drinks arrived, Jana continued, "Well, I've been thinking about making a trip to India for a while and have decided to go this November. Leah is going to go with me, and we will stay maybe for a couple of months."

"I don't understand. You want to go to India and stay there for a few months? Are you serious? Have I caused this to happen because I've been away so much? Jana, I don't have to travel this much. I can make movies locally. I can stay closer to home. I don't understand why you want to do this now, when I've just gotten back and we've been apart for so long."

"That's just it, Michael. We've been apart for so long that our lives have gone in different directions. At least mine has, and this is something I have wanted to do for a long time … even before you went to Italy."

"Why aren't you asking *me* to go with you? Why have you asked Leah? I think you are in love with her and out of love with me. Are you leaving me for her?"

"I'm not leaving you for anyone. It's what I'm going toward, Michael. I love you, and I do love Leah. But I'm going to Ranchi to study the lessons of Paramahansa Yogananda. Leah would like to come with me, and I'm happy not to be going alone. We have decided to sublet the center for a year. We're going to travel around India and also visit the ashram at Ranchi."

For a moment, Michael was unable to speak. "I feel like I am in an elevator that just dropped several floors." He pushed the appetizer away. "And what I am supposed to do while you're away? And you don't even know when you'll be back!"

"You can still continue with your work, Michael, and go forward with your life as well."

Michael asked the waiter for the check then and stood up to leave. "I have to get out of here."

They paid the bill and left. On the way home, Michael lit a cigarette and angrily threw the pack on the console. He drove quickly, parked the car in the garage, and stomped into the house, slamming the door behind him.

Once in the house, he went straight to the bedroom and shut the door. This was a completely crazy notion he had to talk her out of doing, Michael thought.

Jana had trailed behind Michael into the house and now stood at the window looking out at the waves churning in the dark, only the whitecaps visible. She had neither planned nor meant for things to turn out this way. But the longing to leave for India was more powerful than all else. She knew Michael was strong and that he would be okay, but she also knew she had hurt him badly—and that there was really nothing she could do. Around eleven at night, Jana knocked softly on the bedroom door and went inside. Michael was staring at the television and looked as if he'd been crying. He did not look up at her.

Jana explained, "Michael, this has nothing to do with you. I love you very much, but I love God more. It's not easy for me to talk about, and it's difficult to explain. I wanted to tell you so many times but just didn't know how."

But Michael could not understand Jana's desire for God. Over the next few weeks, he wandered dejectedly around the house or left in an angry rage to go to a local bar and come home drunk. He called Jana's father to ask him whether he had known about Jana's plans beforehand.

He called Adi and John to rail against Jana's decision, saying she was "out of her mind." Finally, he called Leah, claiming she was the cause of Jana's decision to go to India. Why couldn't she go to a local group who believed in what she did or just belong to a church? he asked her. The next few months passed in the same fashion, with Michael trying to plead and reason with Jana not to leave and Jana adamant and unrelenting.

Finally, at the end of October, Jana hugged Michael goodbye at the house. They had decided it was too painful to go to the airport together, and Carollyn, who was now running the center for them, drove Leah and Jana to the airport in Providence. From there, the two women flew to Boston and on to Heathrow, with their final destination of Mumbai.

CHAPTER 19

～wwₒₐₑₜₒₒₜₑₒₒ-w～

India

They arrived in Mumbai on the west coast of India at three in the morning on October 31 for a connecting flight to Madras on the east coast. The sights at the airport were primarily of people sleeping on cots, most waiting for other flights. As the plane circled toward its final descent into Madras, Jana was filled with anticipation. Exhausted, she was somewhat irritable and had a headache, but the excitement of the moment heightened her senses. At the arrival gate, garlands of flowers were placed around Leah's and Jana's necks. Immediately, children emerged from everywhere, picking up their luggage and offering to carry it to waiting taxis. These were children trying to eke out an existence for their parents, who watched on the sidelines. Their taxi wound through the streets toward the Hotel Kanchi, allowing the smells of Madras to invade their senses. Streets were teeming with people. Cows leisurely made their way across the road and stopped to eat out of garbage cans along the sidewalk. Later in the evening, Jana and Leah walked down to the ocean, where, on enormous stretches of sand, merchants laid out their wares on blankets and lit candles for as far as the eye could see. It was a staggering sight. Making their way back into the lobby of the hotel, the women were anxious to get to their room. Their day had been overwhelming with their having taken in all the new and different sights.

"I cannot wait to get into that bed!" Jana exclaimed. "It seems like we've been on a plane for days!"

"We have," Leah responded with a weak smile. She walked over to the window to take a closer look at the view. The window was a large open elongated porthole with no screen. The view of Madras was glowing, and Leah could see the city for miles. She decided to take a quick shower before bed while Jana settled in bed under the large mosquito net. Leah discovered that the shower was little more than a faucet with two handles, and there was no division from the counter and mirror on the other side of the room.

The night was quiet, with only the sound of the ceiling fan as they lay under the netting. Jana had decided to read from her spiritual books each night before sleep. She closed the book quietly as the women began to drift off in their new surroundings. Over the next few days, they explored Madras, with its exquisite temples, busy street markets, and bustling traffic. They learned of a beautiful, peaceful vacation spot in the state of Tamil Nadu, just south of Madras, and decided to spend a few days there. The next morning, they rented a taxi and rode along the countryside, observing women on the road in saris carrying baskets on their heads and going about their daily routines. Cows and goats grazed about. In the distance to their right, it seemed that across the whole of India, rice paddies stretched for miles. To the left was the Bay of Bengal.

Arrival in Mahabalipuram was an unexpected oasis from the crowdedness and activity of the big cities. Jana felt immediately that here, at the hotel, all was peaceful and beautiful. No one exhorted her to buy items or give money. She and Leah could walk around enjoying the grounds, the lush foliage, and the Bay of Bengal in the distance.

"Namaste, ladies," their host said and bowed slightly. "I have your room ready. Come—just this way, please."

The women followed and settled into their bungalow on the grounds of the lovely resort hotel and its easy pace. Leah observed that the bed was largely composed of flat slats with a thin mattress on top, best for sleeping. An enormous mosquito net covered the queen-size bed. The smell of burning incense in the evenings, intended to keep away mosquitoes, imprinted in Jana's memory forever.

"I think I will go down for a swim," Jana announced.

"OK. I'm going to do some exploring around the grounds and then catch up with you later."

Jana found that she was the only human occupant sharing the vast Bay of Bengal with the sea life, as if it were her own private swimming place. She experienced a sense of freedom, of space, and of belonging to all that surrounded her. Fishing boats, crude and carved out of native trees, lay in rows along the shoreline, awaiting their masters. That evening, Leah and Jana dined outdoors to the sounds of the ocean, the warm east-India breezes wafting around them. They were happily surprised by a table arrangement the waiter had made out of green stalks and flowers, featuring the word "welcome." They enjoyed a light dish of curry chicken with naan and vegetables. Dessert was caramel custard and Indian coffee. Jana wore a fuchsia top and long pastel skirt with sandals. Leah wore a light blue cotton dress, and she carried a white shawl in case the evening grew cool. Returning to their room a bit later, they crawled under the large mosquito net and white sheet. Jana read for a while and then looked over at Leah. It had been a long time since they had touched or held each other. Jana was aroused by Leah's beauty. She reached out to touch her, and Leah instinctively inched her way over to Jana. They explored each other that night and fell asleep holding each other. In the morning, after they had breakfast, Leah called out to Jana in the lobby.

"Look what I've found!" she exclaimed. Leah was standing next to the hotel's caged pet parrot, Judy, and was delighted to have a substitute pet with whom to converse. Small lizards came for occasional visits to their room. There were all sorts of reptiles and small bats, but the women were not bothered by them. There was something indefinably peaceful and comforting about Mahabalipuram. When the noonday sun became too hot, the women would sit under palm trees and read or nap. One day, Jana and Leah went into the town itself to see the old temples, in particular the Penance of Arjuna, built in AD 700. Amazing sculptures were carved into the temple—of elephants, monkeys, lions, and various gods and goddesses. From atop the temples, the views were magnificent, as the women could see for miles and miles. On the last morning, the women thanked their host for his gracious hospitality and reluctantly returned to Madras.

From there, they flew to Hyderabad, where they were met at the airport by Usha and Vijay, a couple Jana had known when she lived in New York. It was a happy reunion, and Jana introduced them to Leah. They chatted in the back seat as the driver took them back to the house. The Ashoks were relatively well off by India's standards. They had a sturdy brick house with a large entryway and several bedrooms. Usha gave them a tour and then ushered them to a large dining room table, where they had prepared a typical midafternoon Indian luncheon for them. Servants scurried around bringing and taking away dishes of food while the group ate.

"Has Michael finished his film in Italy, then?" Usha asked.

"Yes, he has and is glad to be home for a bit of rest," Jana replied.

Jana told Usha and Vijay about the center she and Leah had created and the kinds of work they did there. Usha was especially interested in the massage work that Leah performed. Leah offered to provide a free massage, to Usha's delight.

"Usha, everything is delicious and so filling," Jana commented.

Leah agreed, adding that she was surprised to find that she enjoyed all the prepared dishes.

Tea was then served with Indian rice pudding. Jana asked Vijay about his work. Vijay said that he had recently retired from his work as a community physician but did make occasional house calls. Usha was working part-time for a travel agency, primarily for enjoyment. Jana then brought out from her room a lovely sari as a gift for Usha that she had selected before leaving for India. Usha admired the fine work and exclaimed that the color was one of her favorites. As Jana and Leah were tired from their traveling, they retired to the guest room for a rest. The beds, as always, were covered with mosquito netting, and a servant had placed burning incense in their room. The following morning, after they had gathered around for breakfast, Usha suggested they go into town for some sightseeing. They were driven to Charminar market, a large open-air market with various kinds of fruits and vegetables, located in the town of Secunderabad. In the afternoon, they went into Hyderabad, where they embarked on a whirlwind of shopping, first at the finer local jewelry shops. Leah selected a 24 karat gold bangle and a ruby ring with tiny diamonds, while Jana was attracted to a pretty pearl bracelet. Jana also selected a gold bangle bracelet for Adrienne and some silver bangles for Camille. They then entered the shops that sold fine saris. Jana chose two, and Leah selected a few for close friends. They could afford just about anything they wanted, as the exchange rate with the rupee was so low. The day went by, and they arrived home thrilled with their treasures and tired from another long day. The following morning, Leah and Jana were treated to a delightful surprise. Usha took Jana and Leah into her sitting room and dressed them in saris of beautiful shades. Their faces were made up as well, and they were adorned with Usha's jewelry.

"Go, go, look in the mirror!" Usha cried.

Jana dutifully went to see how she looked and could not believe her eyes. "I look like I could be attending a wedding or a state event!" she laughed.

She looked at Leah, who was breathtaking. Dressed in a coral-shaded sari of beautiful silk with pink trim, she looked almost Indian herself with her dark hair and the Brahmin mark that Usha had placed on her forehead. When they emerged from the dressing room, the men nodded with approval, and the servant boys stared as they watched the women depart.

"Thank you so much for doing this for us. I haven't felt this elegant in a while," Leah laughed.

"Oh, no, it is my pleasure," Usha replied, "and thank you for the excellent massage."

They were driven off to Usha's mother's home for lunch. She was said to be an ill-tempered, bossy old woman. Jana observed that she was quite demanding of the servant girl who poured water from a cup over the woman's hands as she washed them. The servants were often teenagers from poor villages who came to the towns and cities to live with the wealthier families and work. They went home periodically with money they'd saved to give to their parents. Jana immediately took to one servant, Mira. She was from the village, about seventeen, with a pleasant nature and demeanor. Although normally the servants remained in the background, Jana spent time chatting and getting to know about Mira's life. The gardens were beautiful around the house and the pace very relaxing as the afternoon slipped by. The week went by quickly, but it was not without problems. Arranging flight tickets in India was very difficult, for the schedule constantly changed. Telephoning anyone was a challenge, and frequently Jana was disconnected from Michael or unable to get through. One thing she could not get used to was the fact that everyone, men and women alike, spat in the streets. Continually, the poor came up to Jana and Leah begging for money or asking them to buy their wares. The desperation of poverty was always no farther than right outside one's front door. For Jana, this was heartbreaking to see. But for the most part, she endured the unpleasant aspects of India in stride. On the last morning in Hyderabad, they were woken by a loud rooster, as they had been each morning. They sat at the large dining table and had Indian chai with their breakfast. Then, after the women thanked their hosts for a wonderful visit, the driver took them to the airport for their flight to Calcutta.

While in flight, Jana and Leah began talking about their impressions and observations thus far.

"This is an absolutely fascinating country, isn't it? The patience and kindness of so many of the people I've encountered here is unmatched. But I could never live here, Jana. I've grown so comfortable with all the American conveniences."

"It's true that the culture possesses something America lacks. There is a reverence for life that I have not experienced anywhere else. True, there are barbaric rituals still going on, but the devotion to God is unsurpassed. Many had nothing, but they had God, which was everything."

Jana and Leah were to be in Calcutta for only a short time, as Jana wanted to see the Ganges River, where the multitudes came to pray. They decided to treat themselves to a decent hotel. For only a few more rupees, they were able to stay in relative elegance. They chose the Agosh Ganga Guest House, deposited their things, and hired a taxi to see the Ganges. However, they arrived at the river only to learn that the place where people went to pray was in Benares. Although Jana had learned a little Hindi, she had misunderstood, and they were in the wrong spot. They decided to make the best of it and spent time walking along the riverside, watching some children bathing and men preparing their fishing boats. There was a beverage stand, where they purchased cold orange drinks. After dinner at a Chinese restaurant, the Blue Diamond, they returned to their room exhausted and immediately went to bed. Most nights, they were too tired for lovemaking, but Leah enjoyed spooning with Jana as they fell asleep.

Calcutta was a bombardment of sensation unlike anything either of them had experienced, from the outdoor meat markets and music blasting through megaphones to the sights of the small street vendors showcasing their wares. They walked along narrow streets, looking at huge burlap sacks of cotton, fabric, and shoe repair shops. They visited the Indian Museum, Cottage Industries, which was a lovely shop where they bought some trinkets— soapstone elephants and wooden ones as well. There were terra-cotta bowls and brightly colored boxes. The two also found time for the New Market, where they indulged in Bengali cookies and some new sandals. Everywhere they went, there were boys asking to be their guides, pressuring them to purchase their goods. On the last evening, the women ate dinner at the Park Hotel, where they had salad, chateaubriand, brandy, ice cream, and tea. They flagged down a rickshaw to return to their hotel. Unfortunately, the driver had no idea of the location, and they rode through the streets that night observing families sleeping in the streets with blankets over them.

At last, they were on their way to Ranchi, the place where Jana had longed to visit the ashram founded by Paramahansa Yogananda. Ranchi was located in the mountains, so the elevation made it cooler. As the plane descended, beautiful hills and green farmland could be seen. They traveled by taxi to the ashram, where one of the brothers met them and led them to their quarters. Men's and women's quarters were separate, and Jana noticed that the women's seemed starker than the men's. One room led into another through worn blue wooden French doors. Jana and Leah were ushered into an inner room, where stark twin beds lay alongside opposite walls. The beds were actually long benches with a thin flat mattress on top. There was the requisite mosquito net, a small chair, and a table. The room had no running water, but there was a small mirror and, in an alcove, a toilet. Outside, there were buckets and a faucet for drawing water for washing.

Jana tipped the bottle of Bisleri mineral water to her lips and took a long drink. Having surveyed the accommodations, she decided that they surpassed her expectations for an ashram.

Leah said, "Well, it isn't the Taj Mahal, but not as bad as I thought it might be!"

The women were about to change clothes for dinner when a brother knocked softly on their door to let them know that women were required to wear "frocks" on the grounds. They quickly changed and entered the dining area, which consisted of long low benches and tables. Once again, men and women were separated. It grew dark early and became much cooler. Jana and Leah retired to their room. As they were unpacking, the lights went out suddenly, and they were in total darkness. Blackouts like these apparently happened frequently in this mountainous region, and Jana made her way outside to see what was happening. The entire grounds were pitch-black, and she could barely make out the path in front of her. She turned back and went inside.

"Hopefully someone will come soon with candles or a flashlight," Jana said.

As time went on and no one came, Leah suggested they use a small flashlight she had brought so they could find what they needed for the night.

Lying in bed, Leah thought about where she was— at an ashram in the mountains in the middle of India with her lover. Jana had been distant the last few days, as if preparing to enter this "spiritual experience." It was the festival of Diwali, and as she lay there listening to the music echoing in the distance, Leah felt out of place, uncomfortable. The silence was eerie. She wanted to leave and get back to the cities and sights of India. She couldn't understand Jana's interest in this place or her yearning to get here. As always, there were little lizards crawling around, and knowing that just added to her discomfort.

Morning arrived with the sounds of the roosters in the yard. Jana rose and washed up in the little courtyard, dressed, and went out to meditate. She walked along the path past the gardens and trees. She decided to sit under the tree where Paramahansa had taught his devotees. She had had a longing to be close to God for a long time. It was a longing that neither Michael nor Leah could fulfill. She knew that the ultimate joy, the ultimate peace, would be to find God. Secretly, she had been studying the lessons sent to her each week for years. Now she felt she was ready to move on to the next stage, which included kriya, detachment, and devotion. Part of her also wanted to continue her work at the center because she believed she was helping others and doing good. The thought of no longer working with Leah saddened her. But there was no turning back now. Jana sat and meditated for a while under the cool shade of the trees, surrendering to her future. It was almost lunchtime as she walked back to the room. Leah was lying on the bed reading.

"Hi!" Jana said.

"Hi," Leah replied. "How was your meditation?"

"Nice, thanks. Leah, I know that all of this must seem strange to you and uncomfortable. I probably should not have asked you to come here with me. You could have stayed in Hyderabad or met me in Delhi. I'm sorry. This was something I had to do, and I've known it for a while. This is an oasis, a haven for me—a coming home."

"I understand that, but I feel like you're gradually shutting me out, like suddenly I'm in the way. What's going to happen to us, Jana?"

"I don't mean to shut you out. I would love for you to

be part of what I experience here. Why don't you come to one of the satsangas and see what you think? There's one this afternoon."

Jana explained what a satsanga was, how it was similar to a spiritual lecture, with meditation and discussion toward the end. Leah agreed to join her and see for herself. That afternoon, they sat on cushions on the floor and listened to Brother Anandamoy speak. He was one of Jana's favorite speakers, and she had read many of his talks. He had a great sense of humor, and even Leah laughed at his jokes. The talk was on devotion, and Leah listened intently. Afterward, there was a brief meditation and question time. Leah asked a few questions of the monk about the beliefs of Self-Realization Fellowship. Leah told Jana she was impressed by what Brother Anandamoy had talked about. She did not embrace those beliefs yet admitted she could see what drew Jana to the fellowship. The two women went for a walk around the grounds before mealtime. After dinner, they rested on their cots as the day grew into night, chatting about the self-realization teachings. For a few more days, the women stayed on, savoring the peacefulness and serenity. Then it was time to return to Calcutta.

As a compromise, Jana had agreed to go with Leah on a jungle safari in Nepal, an adventure Leah had selected for them. So the two flew from Calcutta to Kathmandu a few days later. Looking out the plane's window, Jana stared at high white clouds just under the wing and a brilliant sun setting to the west. Upon their arrival in Kathmandu, they were to take a twenty-minute ride on a prop plane to the Gaida Wildlife Camp in Royal Chitwan National

Park. However, there were no planes available, so they settled on a taxi, which would take them up the narrow winding path around the mountain to the summit and the campgrounds. This proved to be an endless journey, circling ever higher and higher up the mountain, where, along the way, they passed Nepali villages, with small children waving at them.

The road was treacherous as night fell. After several hours, Jana inquired as to whether there might be a restroom along the way. Fortunately, the driver spoke some English as well as Hindi and replied that there was one "just farther up." However, *just farther up* came after three more hours and one desperate and unsuccessful attempt at using the bushes along the side of the road. At long last, after seven hours in total, they were met by men outfitted in hats, gloves, and jackets and transported onto a Land Rover to the wildlife camp. At the camp, the two learned there was no electricity. Instead, they used kerosene lamps and candles, as well as a new flashlight they had recently purchased. Wearied, Leah and Jana quickly settled into their bungalow for the night. At this elevation, they found it was much colder. In fact, they were actually in the foothills of the Himalayas. In the morning, Jana awakened to the sound of an elephant trumpeting and for a few minutes searched her memory until she recalled they were in the national park. After an early breakfast, they headed down to the river.

The canoe sliced easily through the waters as the morning sun warmed their bodies. In the foothills of the Himalayas, the weather was about twenty degrees cooler than in Kathmandu. Yet children were still bathing in the river. On the return trip, because of the flow of the current, they rode instead by oxen cart. Through the villages, past small streams, they observed lambs and chickens, as well as naked children waving, bidding them hello, goodbye, or Namaste.

The following day, Leah and Jana received a briefing of tips on how to interact with elephants, including how to feed them "sandwiches." Feeding the elephants sandwiches made everyone laugh. Leah was thrilled to be hoisted up by the elephant's trunk and placed onto his back. They then set out on a jungle safari, with four to a basket. The basket was tied onto the elephant, and they were lifted into it.

"I can't believe we are finally going into the jungle!" Leah exclaimed.

As the elephants slowly began the trek into the jungle, Jana and Leah became filled with anticipation. The first animals of interest, and quite visible, were monkeys jumping from tree to tree. The elephants made their way along the trail while the women had to frequently pull away from trees' thick overgrowth. Soon they were deep in the jungle and could hear unidentifiable sounds that the guides indicated were a particular kind of bird or small animal. A bit later, they came across an angry rhinoceros who did not want to move out of the way for the elephants, so there was a standoff. The rhino finally made a mock charge at the elephant, which easily slid past him. Coming out on the other side of the jungle, the group entered a breathtaking view of open land with tall grass and the Himalayas in the distance.

"What spectacular beauty!" Jana exclaimed. "I can't imagine any sight more beautiful than this one!"

Leah had to agree. "This is more beautiful than I ever could have imagined. Thank you, Jana, for agreeing to do this side trip with me."

As there were no signs of any tigers and no other exotic animals to see, they headed back to camp to get some dinner and hot chai. A few days later, Jana and Leah took another safari but again were disappointed when no tigers were spotted. They were told it was not really the season when tigers came around. Still, both thought it had been an awe-inspiring experience.

From Kathmandu, they traveled on to Delhi, the capital. Here, they visited Mahatma Gandhi's memorial, Raj Ghat, and went to various museums and temples. They took a side trip to Agra to see the Taj Mahal. At the palace of the Taj, one could see the mausoleum that the king had built as a memorial to his wife. The view was magnificent, and Jana imprinted it in her memory. Even more beautiful than being at the Taj itself was the view from the palace. Seeing it for the first time from the palace was like looking at a vast wasteland out of which sprung this stunning vision of east-Indian architecture gleaming white in the sunlight—perfection, thought Jana.

The two women learned when they went into the local markets that they could always find someone to talk to about healing substances. They discovered lovely aromatic oils to use for massages and beautiful scents of incense to use in the rooms of the center. There were always smiling women dressed in colorful saris eager to sell their wares. The only distraction was the constant blare from loudspeakers of Indian music, which sometimes made it difficult to hear or carry a conversation. In one store, Leah discovered a massage bed made very simply with a vibrating and heating mechanism, which she could use at the center. It was not all expensive, and Leah made plans to have three of them shipped back to Rhode Island. The rest of the items were small enough that they could be packed with Leah's luggage. Finally, they looked at beads and bangles that were said to have healing properties. Various metals were touted as containing special powers, and yoga mats were brought out and displayed.

By this time, Leah had shared her feelings of wanting to return to the US. They had been traveling for about two months, and while she was completely mesmerized by India, she felt a pull to return, a longing to get back to her life in Rhode Island and to the center. Jana understood and was grateful that Leah had accompanied her all this time in India. But Jana knew she would go back to the ashram at Ranchi and that the time had come. In the next few days, Leah made plans to fly home from Delhi. She and Jana spent the last days in a hotel in the city while Leah packed up her things.

"It is going to be so incredibly hard to leave you," Leah said, her voice breaking. "I love you so much."

"I know, and I love you. But we can visit each other from time to time. We can write. I would love to get letters from you at the ashram, and I promise to write back. I think Carollyn would be willing to partner with you for a while until you can get someone permanently."

Rather than prolong the pain of parting, Leah decided to leave the next day, and Jana accompanied her to the

British Airways terminal. They exchanged hugs, and both cried out, "I'll miss you!" at the same time. Then Leah gave a wave and went into the customs line. Jana stood there with tears streaming down her face. She felt a part of her had been ripped away. Suddenly she felt lost, confused, and uncertain. Here she was in a strange country where she felt like she was losing her footing. She had arrived so confident and certain of her future. Unexpectedly, she missed Michael—missed home and the center. She would give Michael a call to calm her emotions before flying back to Ranchi.

CHAPTER 20

New Beginnings

After talking to Jana, Michael sat alone in the house on Ocean Drive. Even Rosa had gone. The silence was deafening but for the waves smashing against the jetty. He turned and looked out at the ocean for a moment. It was almost dusk, and he wandered around the empty house feeling at loose ends. He had carefully chosen all that he wanted to take with him back to New York. It had been packed and shipped to his new apartment, which partially overlooked Central Park on the west side. And so he had come full circle. Back to the place of beginnings: where he and Jana had first met, where he had fallen in love, where his career had blossomed. It seemed like ages ago now. He felt the light, the magic in his life, was somehow gone without Jana. It would be like this for a long time, he knew. There would be moments when he felt utterly bereft.

Soon, however, he would be back in the city he loved, the city where he felt alive and exhilarated, unlike any other place in the world. He decided he would get a dog when he returned, like he had always wanted. He would call it Sparkles after the ambience of New York and Jana's irrepressible spirit. Michael took one last leisurely ride around Ocean Drive as the sun cast long shadows on the mansions. There was something reassuring about the steadfast presence of those familiar homes as he turned each bend in the drive.

He was eager to get back to New York and work out the last details. The house was on the market, and the realtor said they would have no problem selling it for a good price, as the home was located on prime real estate. All the proceeds would go to Michael, as Jana had wanted nothing. The apartment in New York was ready to be occupied, the large furniture already delivered. Michael packed up the last of his things and drove down the next day. He wanted to drive. He needed the time to fully make the transition from New England to New York, and the four hours would give him that time to think. As he pulled into the basement parking lot of his new apartment building, it was nearing twilight. Once out on the street, he looked up at the high-rise, noticing many lights beginning to shine in windows above. How he had missed that sign of activity, that pulsing of lives all around and above him. He smiled at the doorman, and the elevator man took him up to the fifteenth floor. He unlocked the door and switched on the light. A warm glow enveloped the spacious entryway. He walked slowly though the rooms of the apartment, seven in all. Then he quickly strode toward the windows—the ones overlooking the park. The streetlamps had begun to glow as he looked over a canopy of green. Michael felt that unmistakable feeling of being home again. Tomorrow he would go look for a dog to walk in the park in the town he called home.

———

Leah's plane touched down at Boston Logan International Airport at about eleven o'clock at night. It had been a long, tiring flight from Delhi to London to Boston. She rented a car to make the drive back to Providence. Leah wanted to get home as soon as possible and sleep in her own bed after having spent months away. She hauled her bags into the trunk and then made her way onto Route 95 South. She had been on the highway for only a short time when she began to feel her eyes closing from jet lag and lack of sleep. Leah thought she would pull over at the next rest stop and grab some coffee. But at that moment, the car hit the guardrail and flipped over twice into a wooded area. The state police were called. Leah's brother, Marcus, was notified of her death and was the one who called Jana. Devastated with grief, Jana telephoned Michael to let him know the news. Then she sat in meditation and allowed the tears to flow. This wasn't a relationship she felt she could share with many people, and the weight of her sadness was overwhelming. Michael, too, felt a sadness as well, for he knew that this was a huge loss in Jana's life.

Jana thought of how Yogananda, as well as many other spiritual leaders, had taught the principles of nonattachment, and their words "God alone" entered her thoughts. Her mind went back to others she had lost, especially Drew, and the pain and suffering she felt for a long time afterward. Now those feelings erupted all over again. Brother Anandamoy had said it best. After all the years a husband and wife spent together, what was there to say at the time of parting? "It was nice, dear. Goodbye." Only God's love was eternal, without betrayal, without conditions, everlasting. She tried to hold to that thought knowing that in time she would be able to let go of this loss as well and eventually live for God alone—in joy, in happiness, and with no expectations, but with every hope that her love would shoot forth from the heart and return one hundredfold. How blessed Jana felt, with beautiful memories and cherished dreams for the future.